Explosive Memories

by

Sherri Thomas

The Matthews Dude Ranch Series

Explosive Memories

Cover Art by *Debbie Taylor*

The Wild Rose Press, Inc.
PO Box 708
Adams Basin, NY 14410-0708
Visit us at www.thewildrosepress.com

Publishing History
First Yellow Rose Edition, 2015
Print ISBN 978-1- 5092-0150-1
Digital ISBN 978-1- 5092-0151-8

The Matthews Dude Ranch Series
Published in the United States of America

"Why'd you tell me your name was Lynn?"

His low voice and breath on her face brought her back to the present. Jordan fought the urge to step back, holding her ground while her knees wobbled, threatening to give out. She wanted nothing more than to stay composed and not be affected by him, but her body defied all reasoning and leaned forward, inhaling his spicy, animal mixed scent.

Irritation flared, and she met his glare with annoyance. "It's my middle name. Jordan Lynn Reece. As for using it, I didn't know you from Adam."

The corner of his mouth tilted up and his eyes darkened. "But we got acquainted real quick."

"As much as you can in the span of twelve hours."

"I memorized every inch of your body, every sound you made…every whimper."

She stumbled back and held up a hand. "Don't."

Trent's gaze shifted to her mouth. His warm palm caressed the side of her cheek. "Why the charade?"

Her heartbeat sped up at his contact. "I didn't think you'd remember me." She cringed at the admission. Damn him and his closeness, and damn her loosened tongue.

His hand slipped to the nape of her neck and massaged the tight muscles. Fighting the urge to moan, she held herself rigid, refusing to let him see how he affected her.

"How could I forget the most fearless, open, passionate girl I'd ever met?"

Dedication

As always…
to my wonderful husband and children

Chapter One

Wicked red and yellow flames licked out of the two-story windows, streaking across the night sky. Glass cracked and shattered. Heat scorched her skin. The smoke chased any trace of oxygen from her lungs. She scrambled through the dense fog, coughing and calling.

They're here somewhere, but where?

Crawling through an open doorway and into a room, her hand connected with a solid form. She scooted closer, peering down at the obstacle in the thick haze. A woman's face so like her own came into view, then a man's crumpled body.

"No. Please no," she cried, reaching out to move hair from her mother's eyes. A sharp pain pierced her heart. Tears streamed over her cheeks as she drew closer to her father.

"Oh, Daddy, I'm so sorry. So very sorry." She bent to kiss his forehead as the ceiling groaned, drawing her attention. "We have to hurry." Tugging on his arm, then her mother's, she swore, "I'll get you out of here. I promise."

A loud crack sounded seconds before the roof crashed down on top of her, burying a scream deep in her chest.

Jordan Reece bolted straight up, heart pounding and breath erupting in short, quick bursts as the horrific accident haunted her.

"You're safe. It's over," she chanted in an attempt to remember the present time.

Sweat beaded out of every pore. Her hands shook as she wrung the digits together and sucked in massive amounts of clean air, fighting to gain control while her body trembled with dread.

She glanced to the clock flashing four a.m. and strangled a cry of frustration. The exact hour of her parents' death. In the beginning, the dreams occurred every night. Over the weeks, months following, the figures lessened until she'd finally been able to sleep a full six hours without interruption.

Why had the nightmare returned? Why after all this time? She hadn't even been home at the time of the fire, but the images never failed to appear crystal clear during her slumber and always ended with the ceiling burying her alive.

Focus.

She needed something to concentrate on, something to draw her attention away from the horror. Staring through the dark in the vicinity of a wall, she wished for the ability to ward off the doom waiting to swallow her soul.

Her dry throat stuck shut as she kicked off the tangled sheets and hurried out of the bedroom. Forgetting the late night journey to her friend's cabin, she stopped short with a hand on the door frame, taking in the unfamiliar shadows. Step by step, careful not to stumble over unknown objects, she inched across the room to the small end table and flicked on the lamp. Light flooded every corner of the combined living/kitchenette area.

Struggling with the loneliness and despair

threatening to suffocate, Jordan advanced to the sink and splashed water on her face. Her mother's lifeless stare flashed, hovering in her psyche next to a picture of her father's twisted body lying on the floor where he fell in desperation to flee the flames of hell.

Jordan swiped an icy palm over her neck to rub away the nervous tension. Her limbs grew colder despite the ninety degree air, and she gripped the edge of the counter for support.

As a registered nurse, she knew the steps to curb the effects of a panic attack—the techniques just didn't always work.

No. This was not anxiety. She'd come too far to permit the weakening of her emotions.

Needing a distraction, she drew the blue and tan checkered curtain back from the kitchen window and gazed into the early morning sky. A blast of stifling air filtered through the screen as dry lightning cracked in the distant horizon. She slid a hand up and down the clammy skin of her arm and shivered as ghosts of the past glided along her spine. The consequences of that night settled heavy on her chest. Bad decisions never to be forgotten.

Bad decisions she continued to make.

She missed the time when her life remained on track, disciplined, and she had known the course of action to keep ahead of hospital politics. Now, after letting one man convince her to give up everything and take a chance, the future appeared bleak. She honestly believed she could make a go of things this time, that he loved her enough for their relationship to succeed. Another error in judgment, but one she thought she had grown enough to handle. She hadn't imagined the end result leaving her jobless and almost homeless, if not for her best friend's generosity.

A rumble of thunder jostled her out of her haze and vibrated the room, followed by an amazing light show illuminating miles of rolling pasture. The storm closed in on the arid Texas range at a startling speed, spraying droplets of water through the screen.

Lugging the glass pane shut, she let the drape fall back in place. Not one to stay still for long, she spent the next few hours listening to the rain pelting the metal roof while unpacking her clothes, hanging the neatly pressed garments in the closet. Anything to eat up the hours until the meeting with Dr. Sheffield, her father's college buddy, and a lifeline to getting her old job back. The physician had been the one who encouraged nursing school and guided her through the process, even giving a star recommendation when the RN position opened at the local hospital.

As day finally showed its full light and the appointment time neared, possessing a need to appear bright and cheery, Jordan selected a yellow sundress. Pulling the cotton over her head, she crossed to the mirror on the wall and inhaled a shaky breath as the reflection mocked her.

Going back to her natural hair color had been one of the many steps to getting her life back, a fresh start. Never would she give anything up for a man again. She ran a brush down the black locks. The strands had been blonde for years, and seeing the transformation harbored many unwanted memories. The person who caused so much grief and disappointment.

No! That girl is long gone.

She was stronger now, older.

Shaking off the unpleasantness of her past, she grabbed her purse. This was the point in her life when she needed to hold her head high and move forward. Determined to make something of herself and make her parents proud, she straightened her spine and unlocked the door…just as the wood sprang open.

"There you are." Darcy Brooks stepped forward, light brown curls bouncing on her gray, short sleeved shirt. "Oh my, God, your hair. I've never seen it so dark."

"I missed you, too." Jordan accepted the hug and patted her best friend's back, a bit taken by an unexpected rush of longing.

Why did I stay away?

Because you trusted an unworthy man.

Because she believed her ex-boyfriend when he told her how much he loved her, how he'd do anything for her, and how he admired the ladylike qualities instilled upon her. So much so, she moved away with him to support his singing career. And by finding a two bedroom apartment and maintaining a full time job while he jumped from gig to gig, she had been able to keep the responsible path she'd carefully planned out for her future. In the end, the joke was on her, letting time and distance separate her from the people who mattered most and truly cared about her. Guilt tumbled through her.

Darcy fingered the tresses. "I love it. It's stunning. Why on earth did you ever bleach it? I like this much better. Your blue eyes really pop."

"And your hair is a lot lighter." She lifted a few of the brown strands.

"Too many hours in the sun." The brunette smiled,

linking their hands. "I wish you'd have let me pick you up from the airport."

"My plane landed later than scheduled, and I didn't want to cause any problems. That's why I texted you saying I'd stay at a motel."

But oh no, her friend had refused to let her spend the night anywhere besides the Matthews Dude Ranch. She'd even kept the porch light lit on one of the cabins to guide the way up the driveway.

"Didn't matter. I couldn't sleep anyway, and it killed me not to rush over here when you pulled up, but Nick insisted I give you time to settle in. He said you'd probably be beat and want to sleep."

Jordan had yet to meet Darcy's fiancé, Nick Matthews, who ran his parents' dude ranch along with his brothers. While she was happy for her friend and grateful to the man who put such a radiant smile on her face, she couldn't help the apprehension sneaking in over this new chapter of her own life.

"He's right. I wouldn't have been much company. You sure it's okay for me to stay? I don't want to intrude on the family."

"Are you kidding? You're *my* family, and this is where you belong. And I don't want to hear anymore on the subject."

"Yes, ma'am." She laughed, relieved to find her friend still considered her family. Not having any living blood relations, they had adopted each other as honorary sisters after a horrible accident landed Darcy in the hospital with amnesia, and Jordan had been assigned as her nurse.

"How was your drive? Did you sleep okay? Do you have everything you need?"

"I realize you're excited, darlin', but give the lady a chance to answer," a deep drawl sounded from the doorway.

Her friend tilted her head with a bright smile for the tall cowboy sporting a snug, black T-shirt and equally tight fitting blue jeans.

Jordan drew her brows together. The man possessed an uncanny resemblance to someone from her past. One who invaded her thoughts and still occupied way too many dreams.

Impossible. She hadn't laid eyes on the man since their one night together. One very long, intense night.

He removed his hat, revealing dark hair and chocolate eyes.

Her throat stuck shut, and she swallowed. Why hadn't she asked more questions concerning her friend's future husband?

Because you were too wrapped up in your own life dealing with one catastrophe after another.

Besides, the answers wouldn't have made a difference. That long ago night, the cowboy never told her his last name. Heck, not knowing him and not wanting her parents to find out where she'd been, she'd given him an alias...had he used a pseudonym as well?

She studied the strong features, noting a dimple in his left cheek which hadn't been present before. The jaw was a bit more square and lacked the presence of a small scar from stringing barbwire. Concluding this was not the man from her past, she sighed with relief.

Boy, what an awkward mess things would've been if he turned out to be her cowboy lover. She laughed to herself. Thank God for small favors—or large ones in this instance.

The man's arm slid around Darcy's waist. Love radiated as he stared down, and Jordan turned away from the intimate moment.

"I'm just happy she's here. Jordie, I'd like you to meet the love of my life, Nick Matthews."

Darcy's voice drew her gaze back to the couple.

"Nick, this is my best friend in the whole world," she continued.

He extended a hand. "I can't tell you how glad I am you're here. All I've heard is Jordan this and Jordan that since you decided to come home." His eyes rolled, but a smile cracked his chiseled features.

She grasped his palm in what her father taught her to be a firm handshake, pumping only once, and letting him withdrawal from the embrace first. "Nice to meet you."

He raised an eyebrow.

Darcy elbowed him in the gut, earning a chuckle as her soulful eyes glanced down at the purse in Jordan's hand. "Were you going somewhere?"

"I was coming to find you in hopes of grabbing a cup of coffee before I meet with Dr. Sheffield about a job." And that was the truth, she just hadn't made it out the door to go in search for her friend, nor had she known exactly where to look.

"You certainly aren't wasting time."

"What can I say, I don't like sitting around."

Too much time to think. Too much time to feel. Must keep going or the ghosts of the past will catch up...again.

"I'll leave you two to talk. Chris's waiting for me at the barns." Nick kissed his fiancée and fingered the brim of his hat as he placed the Stetson on his head.

"I'm sure we'll be seeing a lot of each other." He pivoted and strolled out the door, leaving the wood to bang on the frame.

Jordan swatted her friend on the arm.

"Ow. What was that for?" The brunette rubbed the assaulted area.

"That man adores you."

"I know, but I love him more as the argument goes." Darcy giggled, her face radiating happiness, her eyes bright and sparkling.

What would it be like to feel such contentment? With the direction Jordan's life headed, that was something she'd never experience. She peeked at her watch, noted the minutes slipping away, and glanced up into her friend's frown.

"You *are* in a hurry."

"I'm sorry. I don't want to be late. Dr. Sheffield's only in the office until noon, and he doesn't know I moved back."

"Well then, let's get that coffee." Looping arms, she added, "Make sure you tell him I said hello."

"I will." Having been Darcy's physician during her hospital stay, the doctor was partly responsible for bringing the two together.

"Let's drive my rental to the main house so I won't have to walk back up here." Jordan dug keys out of her satchel and ambled out to the blue Tacoma. Opening the driver's door and getting in, she slid the key into the ignition and waited for her passenger to settle into the leather interior.

"Not a bad deal, huh?"

"Ah ha, I knew you had a deep, dark secret. You're carrying a torch for trucks." Darcy laughed.

Jordan smiled when she really wanted to cringe. That was far from her deepest, darkest secrets. "Actually, I preferred a more practical ride, like a newer car, but this was all they had available."

Putting the vehicle in gear, she laid a heavy foot on the gas pedal. Warm wind blew in from the open window; the air held a familiar scent of animal and wild flowers. Tension in her shoulders drained away.

"You may want to slow down. There's a speed bump right..." The rental bounced hard. "About there," Darcy informed her.

"Sorry." She slowed and continued along the gravel to the main house.

"So, are you going to tell me what happened with Ed-the-Magnificent?"

"Can we discuss him *after* I've sampled a healthy dose of caff—" Swept away by the picture perfect scenery ahead, Jordan stopped in the middle of the drive. "Wow."

The three story, log bed and breakfast resembled a vacationing ski lodge. Glass panes lined the first floor and extended close to the roof on the far end of the inn. Pine trees and mature oaks surrounded one side of the structure with a wooden porch that wrapped around the opposite end from front to back.

"It's gorgeous. I couldn't make much out last night, but...wow." She blinked, trying to take in the whole view.

"I had the same reaction. Park this thing, and I'll show you inside."

Swinging the truck to the gravel area on the right, she killed the engine, fisted the keys in her palm, and exited the automobile.

A golden dog ran up, barking and wagging its tail.

"Hi, boy." Darcy scratched the animal's fur. "This is Dakota, Nick's dog."

Not giving the canine a chance to jump or drool on her, Jordan patted him on the head and sidestepped. She didn't dislike the creature, but the dress cost too much to have ruined by a mud stain or slobber.

A loud whistle split the air, and the animal trotted off in a hurry.

"The guys must be going out on the trails. Dakota likes to lead. According to Nick, he helps desensitize the horses to spooking when the guests go on a guided ride. Honestly, I think the dog just keeps all the other critters away. In turn, there are none to jump out and scare them."

"Everything serves a purpose on a ranch." She recalled the cowboy's words when she'd been curled up on his chest listening to him talk about the animals on his farm. Standing real still, she could almost feel the rumble of his chest on her ear as he spoke in that deep, quiet tone.

A hand touched her arm.

"Hey, you okay? You got a far away look on your face."

Giving herself a mental shake, Jordan nodded. "Sorry, I'm fine. Probably a bit of jet lag."

Wrapping her fingers around the sturdiness of the railing, she followed her friend up the wooden steps to the wraparound deck and entered into a large, pale yellow kitchen. The spacious room sported two large, stainless steel refrigerators, a huge stove, and a round, wooden table in the corner. A robust woman stood at the sink, scowling in their direction.

"Ms. Liz, this is Jordan. Ms. Liz is the ranch cook and makes the best coffee and chocolate mousse cake."

Jordan held out a hand to the square-shouldered lady. "Hello."

"Humph. Might want to get in here earlier if you want a decent breakfast," the cook growled, walking away.

"Her bark's worse than her bite." Darcy grabbed two cups from the counter, filling them with caffeine. "Don't take it personal. Took me six months to get her to even say good morning." She held out a mug. "There's sugar and creamer by the canisters, or if you want flavored, I believe there's several different kinds in the fridge."

"This is fine." Jordan used one spoon to scoop the sweetener and non-dairy product into her cup and another to stir. "Has anyone suggested Ms. Liz loosen the bun on top of her head?" she whispered. Setting the utensils on a napkin, she sipped the brown liquid. The flavor flooded her mouth and awakened her taste buds.

"My thought exactly."

As Darcy laughed, Jordan regarded the future Mrs. Nick Matthews with a bit of envy. "This place has been good for you. You really are happy, aren't you?"

"Nick has been good for me. This place was a bonus." She ambled over to the old, round table in the corner. "I'm even working part time at White's Law Firm in town."

"That's great. I'm glad you found this ranch, and each other." Jordan sat on the wooden chair. Hearing her mother's speech to her about sitting like a lady, she straightened her spine and crossed one leg over the other.

"Okay, spill. What happened with Mr. Wonderful? You were very vague over the phone and never spoke of any problems."

She sighed, wondering where to begin. Deciding on the quick version, she admitted, "Ed only needed me to support him financially while he chased his pipe dream of becoming a country western singer, *and* everything in a skirt." Finding it improper to discuss the dirty details of her relationship, she stopped short of revealing the knockdown, drag out arguments concerning the lack of sex. The man couldn't understand why, after months together, she refused to sleep with him—a detail he envied at one time saying she was truly a lady, and the fact she wanted to wait made her even more attractive…until the clock ran out anyway, and he found other willing females.

"That asshole. After everything you gave up for him."

"I truly think he loved me in his own way. He was always full of compliments."

Ed continuously told her how he loved the fact she always used manners in everything she did, how she never put her elbows on the table or burped or slouched, always ladylike. He often said he loved her outfits and how neat and tidy she kept the apartment. So, she worked every available minute of overtime to help pay their mounting bills, only to hear him say "someday" he'd hit it big, and she could quit her job. Not that she would have. She needed something to do while he spent hours playing in the honky tonks. And he definitely had been *"playing,"* according to the countless women who called looking for him every night.

"Oh, honey, I'm sorry." Darcy reached out and touched her arm. "But I am glad you're back. I hated that you quit your job and moved away. It was like you were at his mercy."

She waved in a dismissive gesture. "I'm over it. Over him. There was something missing."

"Don't ever settle for anything less. Real love does exist. Take me for example. Never in a million years did I think when I applied for a job on this ranch I'd find my soul mate."

But when your heart isn't yours to give, when the past absorbs every cell of your being, and you have to fight each second of the day to stay in charge of the emotions...

"I think I'll concentrate on me for a while. Anyway, I couldn't run right back here. Dr. Sheffield helped me get the job in Nashville, and I owed it to him to stick it out. But Tennessee wasn't for me. I missed home." What part she couldn't be sure. Amarillo offered her nothing, except Darcy and the doctor. Yet, a feeling of belonging enveloped her.

The back door creaked, and a stocky man with an easy smile entered.

"Morning, Sam," Darcy addressed the cowboy.

"Mornin'." He hung his tan hat on the rack and strode over to the coffee pot.

Dark hair, dark eyes, the same shaped face. Jordan's heart rate sped up. Why did every male she came across today resemble *him*. This man was broader, thicker in the chest, and also lacked the scar, but the resemblance to her cowboy of years ago was uncanny.

"Sam, this is Jordan." She turned to her. "This is

one of Nick's brothers."

Chocolate eyes crinkled at the corners as he stepped closer and extended a beefy hand. "The oh so famous Jordan." He bowed, smiling. "You'll certainly improve the scenery around here."

"Sam, behave."

"I mean besides you, Ms. Smarty Pants."

His large fingers engulfed her own. "Hello."

Having seen the two brothers, edginess filled her. Was it possible for a person to have more than one look-a-like out in the world?

"Nice grip." He chuckled, released her hand, and crossed to the counter. "She could give some of the guys around here a lesson in proper handshakes."

"How many brothers did you say Nick has?" Jordan whispered, fearing the answer to come.

"Three."

"What are their names?" Telling herself it didn't matter, she lifted the coffee cup to her lips. Even if the cowboy turned out to be a Matthews, it wouldn't change her course of action. She had no time for the past.

"I can't believe I never told you."

"You've talked about them, but always referred to them as Nick's brothers."

"Well." Darcy frowned. "There's Sam, here."

The cowboy turned around at the mention of his name and grinned.

"Chris and Trent."

Trent. Oh, God. Jordan set the mug down heavier than intended, and the contents sloshed onto her hand. *What were the chances?* And if it was him, would he even recognize her? Perhaps he forgot about her, about that night.

Lucky him. For her, those twelve hours started a spiraling downhill fall. The beginning of many punishments for bad behavior.

From her peripheral vision, she glimpsed the bride-to-be's lips turn into a smug smile.

"They're all very, very handsome and *very* single. Aren't you Sam?" She winked in his direction.

"Don't go trying to pair us off Darc."

"Me?" She laughed.

If she only knew. But few people did. Jordan stole a glance in the cowboy's direction, then back at her friend. "And you know I'm coming out of a terrible relationship."

The brunette sipped her coffee, and with a wink, faced her future brother-in-law. "What are you up to today?"

"Trent and I are headed to town for roofing supplies, then we need to stop by the vet's office. He thinks Sierra might give birth soon and wants to be prepared."

Jordan's stomach somersaulted at the use of her cowboy's name. As much as she longed for the man in her dreams at night, the daytime was another story. She did not need another confrontation from her past. Not now.

"Sierra's one of the mares Trent bred with his prize stallion," Darcy explained, oblivious to her distress.

"Need anything while we're out?" Sam leaned a hip on the counter.

"No, but thanks for asking."

"Anytime. I thought he'd beat me here." Glancing out the window, he straightened. "Ah, there he is."

Alarm bells sounded in Jordan's head. She wasn't ready to face that past. Would he remember? Doubtful. He'd been a twenty-one year old boy with raging hormones six years ago. She, a notch on his belt buckle he probably forgot. But having dealt with the repercussions of their encounter repeatedly throughout her life, she never would forget.

"I should be going. I don't want to be late for my meeting, and I have a few places to stop beforehand." Hurrying toward the door, she gave Sam a quick nod. "Nice meeting you."

"I'm working at the law office this afternoon, but make sure you text me what happens." Her friend crossed the kitchen floor and gave her a hug.

"I will." Jordan spun on her heels and rushed out...only to collide with a very solid chest.

Chapter Two

A familiar spicy, sweaty, male scent invaded Jordan's senses, and she bit back a moan. The years melted away as she struggled for control. No matter how hard she tried, she failed to erase the memory of his touch, the way he'd held her like a precious gift.

Ha. Some gift she turned out to be.

Large hands encompassed her upper arms. "Easy, sweetheart," came the deep, southern drawl.

Two words and goose pimples rose on her skin, and a moment of panic filled her.

Forcing her sights up the six feet plus inches of testosterone to the small scar on his chin to creamy brown eyes, she commanded her brain to focus. "I-I'm sorry."

"No harm." Chocolate orbs narrowed beneath the black cowboy hat, recognition settling on his face as one side of his mouth lifted. "Don't I know you?"

The crooked smile caused a tightness in her chest, and she jerked away. "I'm late."

Sprinting to her truck, Jordan held her breath until she was locked safe and sound inside. With shaking fingers, she inserted the key and turned the ignition three times before the engine rumbled to life. Glancing in the rearview mirror, she inhaled several gulps of air. The cowboy stood on the porch staring in her direction.

Her stomach plummeted. Her skin tingled. Even

from a distance, he affected her.

Best course of action—avoid the sinfully tempting male.

Throwing the gears into reverse, she backed out of the parking area and then drove hell for leather away from the ranch, away from the past, and all the unwanted memories.

****

Trent stared in the direction of the raven-haired woman's taillights. He'd recognize Lynn anywhere, the sway of those tempting hips, the electrifying affect of those blue eyes, those luscious lips.

What was she doing here? And why'd she bolt? Hurrying off without as much as a hello?

Maybe the mystery woman wasn't her. It *had* been quite a few years since he'd seen her; the breasts looked larger, the hair longer. But she felt…like his Lynn.

Maybe the medication caused the hallucination.

He cursed. Most days, he avoided the tablets, but stacking hay and falling asleep in the barn yesterday left him little choice. The searing heat in his shoulder burned as if someone branded his skin with an iron.

Shaking off the illusions, he entered the kitchen.

"What took you so long?" Sam asked, setting a cup in the sink.

Ah, the finer points of his day…answering to his family. "Finishing up a few things," he growled, then nodded in acknowledgement to Darcy as she passed in front of him and exited the room.

Crossing to the table, Trent yanked out a chair and winced as pain ricocheted down his arm. Stars danced behind his lids. The majority of the time, the injury didn't give him much trouble, but this week bore an unusual amount of work with the over abundance of guests vacationing at his family's dude ranch, and chore after chore needing done. He lowered himself onto the wooden seat.

"Trent, we don't have time for you to get comfortable. We were supposed to be on our way to town an hour ago." A scowl formed on his sibling's face.

"Give me a minute." Resting his head in his hands, he inhaled. Why was everyone always in such a hurry?

Boots scuffed on the floor. A heavy hand landed on his good shoulder.

"You okay?" Concern filled Sam's voice.

Damn, he hated when they worried over him. "I'm fine. Just off my mark today." He met his older brother's stare.

"Shoulder giving you problems?" Sam shook his head. "I told you, you were doing too much."

"No." Every day he pressed forward, repeating the steps. The morning meetings at the main house with the rest of the Matthews clan, caring for the animals, taking care of the guests—if any. He ate his meals, fixed fences, showered, swallowed pain medicine if required, and fell into bed exhausted. Just to get up and start over the following day—not feeling anything but physical pain. The struggles with his limb a steady reminder of his past. Two years later and April still haunted him. The night she shot him embedded in his mind forever.

Dating off and on during high school, he knew her better than anyone. Or so he thought. She'd hid the dark side from him well. Friends told him stories, but he refused to believe them until the mood swings.

Fury washed over him. He spent too much time

kicking himself for not seeing her sickness. Too many nights lying awake listening to the sounds, waiting for something to happen.

Trent tightened his jaw and challenged his elder's glare.

"That's why you took meds, right? Don't bother denying it. I can tell by the glassiness of your eyes."

He stood. "Let's go so we can get back and get things done."

"What the hell were you thinking?" Sam rubbed his jaw while scrutinizing him. "You can't work under the influence of muscle-relaxers. Stay here. I'll go to town myself."

"No." Damn it, he was capable of taking care of himself. For too many months, his family coddled him. Not anymore. Two years was long enough.

His brothers had even gone as far as buying him a flat screen television and leather recliner after his first surgery. The gifts were intended to keep him entertained while he healed, but much to his family's displeasure, and the doctor's, the presents failed to keep him immobile for long. He refused to plant his ass in the soft rawhide and let everyone else do the work around the ranch.

According to Dr. Ryhe, his non-compliance was what led to the second and third surgeries. The last one three short months ago. His continual refusal to rest caused the ligaments to tear and the damn thing to dislocate on a regular basis, but he couldn't stop, work was the only thing that kept him going.

"I'm off to Attorney White's." Darcy entered and stopped, glancing from one brother to another. "What's wrong? Something happen?"

"Just Trent being Mr. Hardhead as usual."

His future sister-in-law frowned and crossed the room until she stood in his direct vision. "Is it your shoulder again?"

Great, now she was going to go all motherly. "I'm fine," he said through gritted teeth.

"Too bad Jordan hurried out of here. She could've helped." Her gaze traveled to Sam.

Trent snarled at the two of them. "Who the hell is Jordan? And what does he have to do with anything?"

"*She* is my friend, remember? The one who's staying with us for a while. You passed her on the way in. Black hair, yellow sundress?"

The description fit the woman he ran into. The meds really were screwing with his head. "What's so all fire great about her?" he asked, his tone sharper than intended.

"She's an RN."

Wonderful. "And?"

"Give up, Darcy. Mr. Hardhead isn't going to let anyone help him. He can do everything himself." Sam jammed his hat in place. "I have to go." The door slammed shut behind him.

Hurrying to catch up, Trent grabbed his Stetson and followed to the red F350.

"You aren't working on the ranch today and that's final," his brother informed him when he climbed inside the cab.

"Jesus. Would you give it a rest already? I didn't take a full dose."

Mr. Boss-man swung the vehicle out onto the main road. "Don't matter."

"There's no pleasin' you people. First you hound

me to take the shit, and now you're pissed I did." He reclined in the passenger seat and closed his eyes, shutting out the world.

"I'm not pissed you took the medication. I'm ticked, because you think it's safe to work with them in your system."

"It'll be worn off by the time we get back."

"Yeah…right."

Tired of arguing, he ignored the comment and hunkered down in his seat. He needed to clear his head and relax. Pulling his hat over his eyes, he let his mind wonder over the attractive nurse. Something about the black-haired beauty piqued his interest in a way that puzzled him. A smile tugged at the corners of his lips. The high, round breasts, the never-ending tan legs, the slim waist line that had his hands itching to hold on to the woman for starters.

Whoa, boy, get a hold of yourself.

Showing any interest in his future sister-in-law's friend would create nothing but disaster. Besides, it's not as if he didn't have his pick of the opposite sex if he wanted…key being *if.*

He'd been out a couple of times since the shooting, but only for physical release. Pure and simple. The females he hooked up with knew the score—no strings, no phone call the next day, no chance of exploring a relationship. Bottom line, he'd needed sex.

The last six months of celibacy loomed too long— that explained why the raven hair from long ago had crept into his mind.

"Hey, sleeping beauty, we're home."

The amused voice broke through the haze as a hand shook him awake.

"What? When?" Feeling disoriented, Trent lifted his hat off his face, opened his eyes to an empty truck, and stumbled from the passenger side.

"You dozed off on the way to town. Never even flinched when I shut the door." Sam's voice sounded from the rear of the vehicle.

Wow. He slept through the whole journey?

A high-pitched squeak assaulted his ears as the tailgate lowered.

"You get everything?"

"Yep." Sam tossed a bundle of shingles over his shoulder. "Why don't you take the day off? Not much going on anyway."

"I'm replacing that section of roof on my cabin as planned."

"It wasn't planned. You decided this morning, and you're like a dog with a bone. Once you get your teeth into something, you don't let go."

"You get the supplies from the vet?"

"In the bag." Mr. Authority nodded and trotted off toward the storage shed.

Growing tired of this song and dance, Trent snatched up the remaining sack. Carrying the medical provisions to the horse barn, he stopped and checked on Sierra. The mare greeted him with a whinny.

"How you feeling, girl?" He opened the stall and ran a hand over her body. A few muscles contracted, and she pranced in place. Much to his relief, she didn't appear distressed or uncomfortable.

"I'll be back later."

Exiting the barn, he was surprised at the stillness. Not one sibling in sight. Good. Maybe now he could get down to business without anyone harping in his ear.

24

Crossing to the shed, he lifted a package of roofing materials. His shoulder tightened and pain ripped down the extremity. So much for muscle-relaxers. The medication did nothing but make him tired. Teeth grinding together, he dropped the pack on the back of a four-wheeler parked close by and, as anger fisted inside, punched the wall with his good arm, cracking the board. He *refused* to give in and sit on the sidelines while his brothers handled the ranch.

Grabbing a box of nails and a hammer, he returned to the ATV.

"Trent, wait up."

Groaning at the sound of his eldest brother's approach, he stowed the tools in the compartment under the seat. Swinging a leg over the machine, he crossed his arms over his chest and watched Nick hurry toward him.

"I already let the horses out and fed the smaller animals." Gravel crunched as he stopped in front of the four-wheeler. "So, if you want help…"

Trent readjusted his hat, but kept silent.

"If you need a hand." His gaze wavered. "Hell, I'm screwing this up." He sighed. "Why do I let Darcy talk me into these things. Listen, everyone's worried. You don't laugh. You never smile. I'd feel better if you'd punch something or me, show some kind of emotion."

"Want an instant replay of the last five minutes?" he asked, shaking out the soreness in his knuckles and thinking of the new hole in the wall.

"What?"

Giving a little humph, he grumbled, "How'd you get elected to play therapist?" Not wanting to hear the response, he started the ATV, wishing to forget how dumb he'd been. That was the worst part, being reminded everyday how he mistook habit for love.

Nick reached over and switched off the key. "You ever think I came over here to make amends?"

"For what?" Squinting against the sunlight, he waited for his brother to elaborate.

An uncomfortable silence stretched while his self-appointed shrink stared off in the direction of the pasture. Talking like this bordered on unnatural, but since Darcy entered the picture, more and more the love struck groom-to-be embarked on these meaningful conversations.

Had *he* been as sappy when he'd dated April?

No. Just young and dumb. Walking around in a haze of glory, carefree, with a willing woman on his arm—who manipulated every minute of his...

"I saw the changes in April, her erratic behavior. I chalked her moods up to moving in here and the pressures of the wedding. I never once imagined a chemical imbalance." Nick's gaze cast downward, then shot back up. "Let me help you with the roof, because I'm your brother."

"Not because you feel sorry for me?"

He grinned. "There are a lot of reasons to feel sorry for your ass, but no."

Fighting a smile, Trent started the four-wheeler. "Meet me there," he yelled over the roar of the engine and drove to the cabin, feeling the weight of the last few weeks tighten his neck muscles.

Between the conversations with Darcy, the concern on his mother's face, and now Nick, he grew ashamed of the way he'd treated them. Today may be as good a time as any to set things right. In all honesty, he grew tired of driving the people who loved him away and thanked his lucky stars the clan still spoke to him after the way he treated everyone. Since the surgeries, he made a job out of refusing their help. A fact his future sister-in-law pointed out a couple of days ago, and she didn't mince words.

Hauling bundles of shingles on his uninjured shoulder up the ladder to the roof consisted of no small feat, and he almost wished someone would stop him. The family wasn't to blame for his lack of better judgment now or earlier. Dating April on and off during high school, he ignored the warnings, the nagging voice telling him something was off, and jumped to the next logical step—asking her to marry him. And when his parents asked him to pitch in more with the ranch, to do a bit of traveling to pick up new horses and such, she became irate. The fight they got into after he returned with the ranch's newest bull was the worse night of his life. An evening that almost ended it all.

The rattling of the ladder broke into his thoughts as Nick's face popped up from the side of the roof.

"Took me a little longer than I expected to get back here. Throw me those nails, and we'll get this done in no time."

Together, they worked side by side for hours, tearing off the old, damaged portion and replacing with new; the pounding of the hammer filled the silence.

Sweat dripping from his forehead into his eyes, Trent stripped off his shirt to wipe his face. Catching sight of a dark blue Tacoma parking at Darcy's old place, he stared as long, tan legs swung out of the vehicle. From his location, he observed the top of the tan cowboy hat followed by the familiar yellow sundress from this morning.

Jordan glanced up and stared back before reaching into the truck and pulling out a couple of bags.

"Don't let your past ruin chances in your future," Nick's voice came from beside him.

"April didn't cripple me."

"I've seen you pull back when a female shows interest." His brother's feet shifted.

Swaying hips disappeared inside, and he faced his wannabe therapist. "Not that it's your business, but I've been with women since."

"I don't want you to miss out because of *her*."

"Darcy's made you soft."

A chuckled filled the air. "At one time, I would've knocked you on your ass for that comment, but you're right...to a degree. I'd give her the moon, if I could. She's worth that, and a whole lot more."

Trent reflected on the conversation while cleaning up and checking on Sierra.

"I'd give her the moon, if I could."

He never experienced such a strong sensation. Not even with April.

Too bad he figured that out *after* she shot him...twice.

Chapter Three

Jordan glanced in the mirror for the hundredth time later the following day. She swiveled one way then the other, checking the fit of the new jeans. The material felt foreign against her skin. She hadn't worn denim in years. Not since her parents' deaths. The basic clothing had represented a careless, ungrateful, partying teenager from the past.

The idea of purchasing the clothes hovered on the bottom of her list, but as Darcy stated in a text message, wearing slacks and dresses around the ranch would never work. The designer outfits were impractical and sure to get ruined. Not to mention the sandals and flip flops that would in no way protect her feet from the elements.

Not wanting to draw attention, or go into a personal explanation, Jordan gave in and also bought a pair of boots.

The ringing of her cell phone ended the modeling in the mirror, and she snatched the device off the dresser. "Hello."

"Wanna have supper with me?" Darcy's voice filtered over the line. "Give me a chance to redeem myself for leaving you on your own last night and today."

Jordan glanced at her watch. Six already? "Where?"

"At the main house. We can talk about your meeting with Dr. Sheffield."

"I..." Would Trent be there? She wasn't ready to see him. Not yet. Not until she figured out the best way to handle *that* situation. But she moved back home to be closer to Darcy, not avoid her. "Give me a couple of minutes."

"Okay. See ya in a few."

Jordan checked her mirrored image once more and frowned. Making a snap decision, she scurried out of the denim, donned a pair of gray capris, a burnt orange blouse, and a pair of sandals before heading out. The outfit may be impractical around the barns, but deemed appropriate for supper.

Walking in the warm air, she breathed deep until a calmness washed over her. A cow mooed in the distance, drawing her attention. Other than a herd or two of animals in the pasture, the land appeared vacant from the human standpoint.

An edginess clawed at her insides as she reached the porch, and her heart rate accelerated as she climbed the stairs. "Please don't let him be in here," she whispered.

Seeing only her friend through the screen, her pulse slowed a bit, and she tapped on the side of the door.

Her hostess crossed the kitchen and opened the barrier. "You don't have to knock."

Letting the wood shut behind her, she smoothed a palm over her thigh. "I'll try to remember that."

"The guys are going to be late. One of the mares is in labor and having trouble." Her perky friend grabbed plates and silverware. "So, we're going to start without them."

"If you'd rather go down there and help, I can find something on my own." She relaxed with the knowledge of not having to face Trent.

"No way. I feel bad enough for deserting you already. Besides, I'd only be in the way." She strolled over to the table and uncovered the rectangular dish in the center.

A spicy aroma filled the air, and Jordan's stomach growled as a reminder she'd gone the entire day without eating.

"Ms. Liz has tonight off, but she fixed a killer Mexican casserole. Come on, dig in."

"Smells wonderful."

"I even bought your favorite wine on my way home today." Darcy opened the refrigerator and produced a bottle. "To celebrate your return to Amarillo."

"You know I don't drink very often." She'd given that up before she was even of legal age.

"Oh, come on. I recall you enjoying a glass or two when I lived with you, and this is to celebrate your homecoming. One glass won't hurt." Her eyebrows dipped in the center. "You aren't an alcoholic are you? Oh, God, I'm sorry. You never said anything. Forget I even asked."

How easy it would be to go along with that story. But unable to lie, and feeling like a heel, Jordan shook her head. "I'm not an alcoholic. And you're right, one glass would be fine," Jordan said so as to not hurt her friend's feelings. She recalled the two occasions her friend referred to. In order to avoid an explanation, she had poured the alcohol down the drain periodically when Darcy wasn't looking to make it appear as if she'd been drinking. Being a respectable, proper woman wasn't easy, but she held close the promise she made to her deceased parents.

Changing the subject, she asked, "Where are Mr. and Mrs. Matthews?" She'd had the pleasure of meeting Nick's parents once during her employment at the hospital when his dad came in for scheduled tests.

"Sailed out a couple of nights ago to explore the ends of the earth." Darcy grabbed two goblets from the cupboard and poured a generous amount of wine in each.

"You mean she's still dragging that poor man around the globe?"

"He's convinced her to calm down on the traveling, even managed to stay here for the past three months before she whisked him away again." The plates were set on the table. "If not for Trent's surgery, I doubt he'd have succeeded. I think she uses her husband's health as an excuse to tour the world."

"Trent had surgery? For what?" The questions exploded out of her mouth before she reined in her thoughts.

"The screws needed replacing in his shoulder," she answered, handing over one of the glasses. "He had problems with a torn rotator cuff in the past, and the dang injury doesn't want to heal."

Jordan's mind absorbed this information and kicked into nursing mode. She wondered if he listened to the doctors or went to therapy. Perhaps Sam drove him there yesterday.

Her friend pulled out a chair and sat. "I'm sorry about last night and today. The last thing I wanted was to leave you by yourself the minute you arrived."

"It's not like I haven't been by myself before," she stated.

Darcy placed a spoonful of casserole on each plate. "Still, I feel horrible. Mr. White has a big case out of town in a couple of days, and I was elected to get everything together before he left." She rolled her eyes. "The good news is, with the exception of running in to check phone messages, I'm off until he returns." She smiled. "I do have to work around here, but that's more fun than anything."

"Speaking of fun, have you and Nick set a wedding date yet?" she asked, scooping up a bite of food. Her eyes watered as the hot spices swarmed her taste buds. She blinked several times to hold the tears back, and tried to focus on Darcy's answer.

"No." The bride-to-be sighed. "Well, kind of. I don't know. If it was up to him, we would've eloped months ago, but I can't do that to his parents. Tammy'd never forgive us."

Grabbing a napkin from the center of the table, she dabbed her mouth and sucked in air. "Mind if I get some water?"

"Help yourself. Glasses are in the cupboard by the window."

Jordan rose and proceeded to get herself a drink. After taking a swallow to douse the flames, she repeated, "So, when were you thinking?"

"Second or third week of September. The ranch has fewer guests after Labor Day, and we won't feel guilty leaving the others shorthanded."

"That's not far away." She placed her tumbler on the table in front of the wine, nudging the alcohol back an inch.

"I know, but this place picks up again in late October and…" A devilish glint sparkled in her eyes. "Nick won't wait much longer. He wanted to be married months ago, but time got away from us, and the ranch was booked solid, and well…" She shrugged. "…here we are."

"Have you decided on colors or flowers?"

Her friend nodded. "I want to keep everything simple. I'm thinking maybe roses or carnations or maybe some sunflowers. Okay, so I can't make up my mind. Help me?" she pleaded with a smile.

Uncertainty flowed through Jordan, but wanting to be there for her best friend won out, and she chuckled to cover the hesitation. "I'm not sure how much help I'll be, but I'd love to." Biting into a spicy layer, she grabbed the cold liquid again. "Wow. Ms. Liz likes the spices." Her mouth burned, yet she couldn't stop eating the delectable food.

"That she does." Darcy laughed not showing any signs from the excessive heat she shoveled into her mouth.

"How can you eat this stuff without guzzling a gallon of water?"

"I'm use to her cooking, I guess."

Eyes tearing up again, Jordan dabbed at the corners with the cloth and added, "How about mums and sunflowers, keep with the fall season? I saw pictures in a magazine of a wedding up north, and the outcome was stunning."

Darcy tapped her lip with the fork. "Ya know, I like that, and if the local greenhouses don't have the right arrangements, I'm sure we can find something close or even fake ones. It's worth a shot." She lifted her wine. "Here's to fall flowers and praying we find the perfect ones."

Jordan raised her goblet and saluted before bringing the alcohol to her sealed lips, making it look as though she took a sip. She knew the deception was wrong, but things were just easier this way. Too many bad memories associated with drinking, too many bad decisions. All better left buried in the past.

"Okay, enough about me. How'd things go with Dr. Sheffield?"

Frowning as she set her drink down, she gave a deep sigh. "Of course, my position was filled, and right now, the hospital is overstaffed. Once the board shifts everyone and weeds out the workers from the slackers, there may be an opening. Doc promised to speak to the board on my behalf, but there's no guarantees." No way was she going to voice his concerns surrounding her bouncing from job to job and now living on a ranch.

Geez, she felt like a teenager again listening to his worries. She rubbed the crease of her brow with her index finger.

His first comments bordered on how her parents would be so proud, then he asked where she was staying and things went downhill. Watching her grow up, he knew how horse and cowboy crazy she'd been as a teen, recklessly crazy. The way he saw her track record, she already gave up an RN position to follow one man, what reassurance could he give his supervisor when he himself worried she'd fall back into old habits.

"He promised to call when a job comes about." She cringed. "You might be stuck with me longer than intended. I mean, if it's okay with you and the Matthews?"

"You can stay as long as you wish. I'm sure Nick will feel the same."

"What about the others?"

"We spoke to everyone before offering the cabin. No one had any interest in using the place. In the meantime…" She smiled. "I have a proposition for you. Nick and I were talking and wondered if you'd consider working on the ranch? It'd be great to have an RN on site, especially if we start having kid groups stay." A sheepish grin lit her face. "The idea really was Tammy's. She's thinking of hiring a nurse for the 'just in case' situations, and I told her you were moving back. There's always a medical emergency of one kind or another."

Jordan laughed. She couldn't help it. The future Mrs. Matthews bulldozed right through the speech.

"What's so funny?"

"I think you've spent too much time with Nick's mom."

Darcy chuckled. "You're right. She does have a habit of going on and on to get things the way she wants. Sorry. I didn't mean to blindside you. Once the idea presented itself, I ran with it, and I'm sure you've had your share of ranch emergencies growing up in Amarillo."

"I grew up in Lubbock," she said absently around another bite of the spicy supper.

She moved the food around on the plate with her fork. The job offer was a pleasant surprise, but with Trent close by, she questioned the logic of accepting. On the other hand, she couldn't go much longer without a paycheck. Sure, a small portion of inheritance from her parents' passing remained in the bank, but she dipped into those funds way too much as of late.

"You never told me." A frown lined her friend's mouth as she scooped a bite of food into waiting lips. "Come to think of it, you haven't volunteered much information regarding your past."

"Not much to tell that you don't already know. I grew up a couple of hours from here and moved to Amarillo two and a half years ago when Dr. Sheffield offered me a job at the hospital. Maybe someday, when you're bored, I'll fill you in on all the exciting details." She laughed out right. "Anyway, thank you for the job offer. Can I sleep on it?"

"Of course. Take as much time as you want. I do have to tell you, you'll have to help a bit with the animals and guests if you take the job. Not as much as the rest of us, because your first priority would be nursing, but during the down times." Her friend leaned back. "Man, I'm stuffed. If I keep eating this way, I'm going to need new jeans." She stretched and glanced at Jordan's outfit. "Speaking of, did you go shopping like I suggested?"

"Yes."

Brown eyes narrowed at her from across the table.

"I swear. I figured these"—she motion toward her capris—"would be okay for supper. It's not like I'm traipsing around the barns."

"True. You just always dress so impeccable. I wasn't sure if you'd even consider wearing jeans and T-shirts." Darcy sipped her wine. "Speaking of...you want to go horseback riding tomorrow?"

A weight settled on the center of her chest. "I haven't ridden in quite a while."

"You ladies save us any food?" a deep voice called

as the door creaked opened.

Jordan turned toward the voice and suffered a bout of tunnel vision as her sights zeroed in on the one cowboy who tied her nerves in knots. Heart pounding, she waited in the deafening silence for him to speak, doubting she'd hear anything above the buzzing in her ears.

Trent placed his hat on the rack along with his brothers and joined the group, washing up at the large, two-sided sink.

She inhaled and put a hand on her stomach to quell the nausea. What gave him the right to be so calm, to look as handsome as he did all those years ago?

"Nope. We ate it all." Her friend got up and grabbed plates.

"You don't have to do that, sweetheart. We can wait on ourselves." Nick kissed his fiancée's cheek.

"I know."

"Don't knock it, big brother. From what I hear, once the honeymoon is over, you won't get her to do a thing for you."

Pulling her gaze from the man who unknowingly changed her world, she observed the shortest Matthews brother who'd mumbled the comment under his breath. Not that he was vertically challenged. He still topped her five foot six frame; he was simply shorter than the others.

"For that you can get your own supper." Darcy placed one dish back in the cupboard and laughed when he groaned.

Sam chuckled. "That'll teach you to keep your trap shut."

Jordan found it difficult to concentrate on the

banter when her stomach churned with uneasiness. From the way the men stood, Trent failed to notice her. What would he say when he turned around?

Butterflies the size of birds swooped down in the pit of her belly.

"How's Sierra?" Her friend placed the plates on the table. "That's the mare in labor," she informed Jordan.

"Momma and colt are doing great."

"She had a boy? That's wonderful. I know y'all hoped for a stallion." The brunette wrapped her arms around Nick; her face beamed with excitement as she placed a lingering kiss on his lips, earning wolfish whistles from the others.

"Grow up," the eldest reprimanded without releasing his bride-to-be.

"A leg was hung up, but once we adjusted him, she gave birth like a champ." The unknown brother told her as he crossed to the table, plate in hand.

The men advanced, and Jordan bit her lip. The anticipation over the next few minutes circled in her chest. Feeling as though she was free falling off a large cliff, she grabbed the edge of the table.

"Chris, I don't think you met my best friend, Jordan," Darcy introduced, extracting herself from her fiancé's arms. "Chris is the odd ball and lives here in the main house."

"Why move into one of those small cabins when I have this whole place to myself. Unless of course Mom and Dad are in town or we have guests, but hey, even then, I have the whole right wing." He reached out to shake her hand. "Nice to meet you. She talks about you constantly."

"That's reassuring." Jordan pried her fingers from

the wood and gave his hand a squeeze.

"And don't believe everything you hear about me. It's only half-true." He winked, holding her hand a second longer than the other two brothers had.

Letting go, she nodded in acknowledgement and peeked over at the remaining cowboy.

Here it comes…the moment of truth.

Please don't let me embarrass myself by passing out. Because right now, that was exactly how she felt.

"And I believe you ran into Trent yesterday morning," Darcy continued.

He stood by the island where pots and pans hung from the ceiling, his smile falling to a frown as his eyes narrowed. "Jordan?"

Without a word, he stepped forward and his palm connected with hers, swallowing her fingers in a warm, tight grip. An electrical shock tingled up her arm.

Skeptical brows narrowed. "Jordan?" he repeated.

"Hello." She met his confused gaze. Keeping her feelings under control deemed no easy feat. Years ago, she'd given herself to this man and lived through hell because of the misguided actions. Now, it was all she could do to remain in her seat.

A throat cleared.

"You gonna eat or stand there all night gawking at the company?" Sam winked in her direction and brushed past Trent.

Jordan withdrew her hand in haste, grabbed her wine, and without thinking, took a long sip. The liquid traveled down her throat to her belly, landing in a pool of acid.

The cowboy straightened. "Just waitin' on y'all to get out of my way." He yanked out the empty chair and straddled the seat beside her.

She glanced around at the others, wondering if anyone would notice if she made a bee-line for the door. Catching Darcy's eyebrows raised in question, she sighed and resigned herself for a long evening. Of course, her friend would care and be suspicious as to why she hurried out of there, which ended her internal debate. She tried mentally to remove herself from the situation. A tactic she used as a child whenever she wished to be someplace other than with her parents.

But this time, her imagination failed to engage her fully as a spicy male scent wafted over her senses. A thigh brushed hers, leaving heat in its wake.

Not wanting to draw attention, she placed a bite of food in her mouth and shifted away at the same time.

Funny how the once fiery-hot casserole now tasted bland. Her gaze rose yet again and caught the grim yet knowing frown on the handsome face to her right. She reached for her water, and over the next half-hour, played with the remaining food on her plate, refusing to look at the man crowding her space.

The glass of wine drew her attention more often than not, mocking the years she'd gone without. Maybe the liquid would help get her through the night…

Trent's shoulder brushed hers. A tingling swirled from the limb to her toes, and she sucked in a breath. What the hell—anything had to help at this point. Grabbing the goblet, she drank a healthy swallow then another, with less guilt than she expected at breaking her vow. Her limbs relaxed a little more with each taste. The notion of excusing herself filtered in and out, but every time she got up enough nerve, Darcy pulled her into whatever conversation was flying around the room.

Not sure if her answers even made sense, she observed the others, her attention pausing on the one person responsible for her discomfort.

Their gazes caught.

Trent shoved the plate of half-eaten casserole away as the legs of his chair scraped the wooden floor. The air snapped with tension as he stood and stared down. "You ready to end this charade, *Jordan*?"

All conversation ceased, and she froze.

"Trent, that's no way to speak to a guest," Nick scolded.

The brothers made eye contact for a split second. "I used to know her."

"Used to?"

She fisted her hands, digging her nails into the palms. Five pairs of eyes fell on her, and heat crawled up her neck. Oh, how she'd give anything to be anyplace else right this moment. Why did he have to do this *now?*

"We met at a bonfire over at Charlie's the weekend he graduated."

"You mean *she's* the one you spent the night with. The reason April—"

"Shut up, Chris."

Apparently, his family knew all about her *and* their night together. Humiliation struck hard, and her heart skipped a few beats. The wine and acidy food swirled in the pit of her stomach, getting ready to erupt. Bile rose in her throat, causing her to breathe deep through her nose.

"Ah hell," Sam exclaimed, tossing his napkin on the center of the table.

How could she even begin to explain the past to

these people? More importantly, how would she explain to *him*?

Her gaze found the familiar brown one from that precious night long ago. Panic edged its way in, and breathing became difficult.

Trent held out a large palm. "We need to talk, *Lynn*."

Chapter Four

Not wanting to have this conversation in front of the whole family, Jordan rose as Trent seized her hand.

"Lynn? Who's Lynn?" Darcy asked, following the pair to the door. "What's going on?"

"Darc, let them go. I'm sure we'll find out soon enough." Nick's voice filled the room behind them.

Heart hammering in her chest, Jordan hurried down the steps and across the yard. Not that she possessed much choice with her fingers tucked in the cowboy's tight grip.

"Will you stop? Or do you want me to break my ankle?" With great effort, she pulled her hand from his.

He glanced to her sandaled feet and adjusted his pace.

"Where are we going?"

"Someplace to talk without bein' interrupted," he answered, his drawl thick.

Some time ago, she loved how his southern tone intensified when he was aroused; apparently this rang true when he was upset as well. She'd loved listening to him talk while laying side by side in the back of his pickup, loved the feel of his chest rumbling when he laughed, loved the feel of his naked body next to hers.

Jordan shook off the recollection. Traveling down memory lane wasn't a road she wanted to visit, but had a feeling in the next few minutes, the choice wouldn't be hers.

"Key." He stopped at her cabin, holding out his hand.

"It's not locked." She stepped past him, opened the screen and interior door before entering the living room. The sound of the latch clicking shut echoed in the silence.

Trent raised a hand to his hair and frowned.

Taking a guess at what he was looking for she commented, "Your hat's at the house."

His hot gaze shot through her as he stormed to the sink and splashed water on his face. Tan hands braced on the edge of the white counter as he bowed his head. His muscular back flexed with the movements.

Why was he distraught? He wasn't the one facing the firing squad. Or had he somehow found out…

Does he know?

Feeling a bit too warm, she pulled at the collar of her shirt.

"Why a fake name?" His voice filled the room, but he kept his back toward her as he stared out the window. "It's not like we ended things on a bad note. And why didn't Darcy tell me I knew her best friend?" He turned around.

Being face to face, staring him in the eye, she wasn't sure how to explain or how much she needed to explain. "I don't make a habit of giving people a rundown of my past."

"I got the impression you and Darcy are close?"

"We are." Her hands turned cold, and she clasped them together. "And not once had you mentioned your last name."

"Neither had you. Not to mention you lied about

your first." He pinched the bridge of his nose. "Back there in the kitchen, why'd you pretend we were strangers?"

Straightening her spine, she countered his question, "Why'd you go along with it?"

His low voice captivated her, as did the small scar along his jaw and slow swagger as he started across the room. The years dropped away...

Jordan remembered being nervous the day her and her friend, Rachelle, attended that party a couple of hours from home. The afternoon sun blazed hot, and she hadn't known anyone there. Someone handed her a beer, and the alcohol felt good going down her parched throat. After drinking the courage in a bottle, she found herself letting loose and dancing in the back of a white pickup truck until a sexy cowboy helped her down and into his arms. When Rachelle had wanted to leave so they wouldn't miss curfew, she wasn't ready to go. Choosing to disobey her parents, yet again, she stayed at the party with Trent. Someone who let her be herself. Someone who made her feel special.

But if I'd been home at curfew, I could've saved my parents.

"Why'd you tell me your name was Lynn?"

His low voice and breath on her face brought her back to the present. Jordan fought the urge to step back, holding her ground while her knees wobbled, threatening to give out. She wanted nothing more than to stay composed and not be affected by him, but her body defied all reasoning and leaned forward, inhaling his spicy, animal mixed scent.

Irritation flared, and she met his glare with annoyance. "It's my middle name. Jordan Lynn Reece.

As for using it, I didn't know you from Adam."

The corner of his mouth tilted up and his eyes darkened. "But we got acquainted real quick."

"As much as you can in the span of twelve hours."

"I memorized every inch of your body, every sound you made...every whimper."

She stumbled back and held up a hand. "Don't."

Trent's gaze shifted to her mouth. His warm palm caressed the side of her cheek. "Why the charade?"

Her heartbeat sped up at his contact. "I didn't think you'd remember me." She cringed at the admission. Damn him and his closeness, and damn her loosened tongue.

His hand slipped to the nape of her neck and massaged the tight muscles. Fighting the urge to moan, she held herself rigid, refusing to let him see how he affected her.

"How could I forget the most fearless, open, passionate girl I'd ever met?"

Ha. That girl was long gone. Life's harsh lessons sucked the innocence right out of her...leaving barely a shell of a woman behind. She dropped her gaze. This time, she had to make the right decisions.

He nudged the underside of her chin with a bent finger and gave a lopsided grin. "I'm kind of fond of the girl who stripped off every scrap of clothin' and dove into the pond with my headlights lightin' the way."

Again, that night flashed back...

After Rachelle left and the bonfire died down, Trent offered to take her home, but not wanting to face her parents or end the fun, she declined and spent hours in the man's arms, talking, laughing, learning his body.

The next morning, she had him drop her off a few blocks away from her house, saying she needed to visit a friend before going home. When in truth, she didn't want her parents to see her getting out of a man's truck. Though he gave her his number, in all the confusion following that day, she wasn't sure whatever happened to the slip of paper.

A calloused thumb stroked her bottom lip, bringing her attention back to the present and his mouth hovering above hers. His breath caressed her skin.

Energy radiated off him in waves. "We could pick up where we left off."

Trying desperately to disentangle herself from the trance he wrapped around her, she moved to put space between them. "N-no."

"You don't sound so sure." He moved closer, and large palms bracketed her face as his lips grazed hers in the barest contact. "This feels good. You feel good." His fingers treaded into her hair as he crushed her mouth with raw passion and teased the seam of her sealed mouth with his tongue.

Jordan's knees threatened to buckle, and she grabbed a fistful of his shirt. Shame and uncertainty melted into the heat of his kiss, sweeping her up. Shaking and lost in the need for comfort, she let him carry her back to those blissful hours. She wanted to be absorbed into his skin. To quiver with excitement the way he'd made her do in the past. To forget the heartache of seeing the pile of ashes where her home once sat. The tragedy in the following months. The guilt. The heartache. Even for a split second.

She shoved aside the anguish flowing deep and reveled in the building passion. Strong hands roamed over her hips, up and down her back, guiding her closer until no air circulated between their bodies. He moaned and seized possession of her in every way.

Terrified that dreadful morning would invade her mind, but also afraid he'd stop making her feel alive, she clung to him. He made her lose her head and want to be the wild girl he once knew.

But she was an adult now, capable of controlling her hormones, and she refused to go back in time.

Jordan flattened a hand on his chest. "I can't do this," she mumbled, tearing away and rushing to stare out the window into the night. God, his hot skin felt solid and strong. She rubbed her hands together to rid the feel of his body. "I'm not the same person. I can't be her." She was stronger now, which was why the panic attacks happened in the middle of the night when she was most vulnerable.

"I'm not asking you to be anyone you're not."

A bitter laugh slipped from her lips before she could stop it. How could he cause her to doubt everything she stood for in the span of two seconds? One touch and bam, she couldn't remember her own name. "You're asking a lot more than that." Coldness enveloped her as she wrapped her arms around herself. "I've been someone I'm not for so long, I don't know who I am anymore."

"I know the feeling."

She glanced over, and the compassion in his features shocked her. When was the last time someone listened? Really listened to her? Understood her? Held her? God, she wanted Trent to hold her in the worst way. For him to be all she made him to be in her mind.

Unable to give in to her desires, she perched on the

edge of the couch. *You're stronger than this. You do not need a cowboy to hold you up.* She pulled her armor back in place and straightened her back.

"Maybe we can help find each other." He settled on the sofa and leaned forward, his leg brushing hers. "What's the harm in that?"

"A lot." Feeling his gaze, she lowered her sights to the floor.

The silence stretched until she was sure she'd explode from feeling him next to her, feeling the inquisitive stare.

"I looked for you."

Her stomach swooped downward. If he'd discovered what happened in the months following, surely he'd have confronted her...wouldn't he? She searched his face for a clue. If she reflected on the outcome of their night together, she'd go on overload for sure.

"No one knew the mysterious girl who blew in and out of my life. I guess if I'd known your real name, maybe I'd have gotten answers, huh?"

Realizing he never found out about her condition, she relaxed her tight shoulder muscles a fraction. Still, by not giving him her given name, she not only protected herself needlessly from her parents discovering her whereabouts, but she also prevented him from locating her.

She'd asked about him, too. Turned out Rachelle didn't know the gang at the fire. Her *friend* had overheard a group at the mall discussing the bonfire and, always one for adventure, happened to get directions from one of her acquaintances.

Weeks later, Jordan even found herself driving

around trying to find the shack where she'd spent the night with the very hot and sexy cowboy, trying to find one last sliver of sunshine in her increasingly darkening world after the last night she ever disobeyed her parents. The weeks following her parents' death, life as she knew it tumbled out of control. Having nowhere to go, she moved in with her only living relatives.

What a mistake.

He fingered a strand of hair on her shoulder. "You told me you wanted to live on the edge. You never wanted to grow up."

"Yeah, well, we all know that's not possible." Not able to sit close any longer, she sprang to her feet and fled to the kitchen window. She stared out the glass toward the barns as the last shadows disappeared behind the rolling pasture.

After a few moments, she inhaled a deep breath and faced him.

Trent observed the anguish in Jordan's beautiful face. Time and maturity sharpened her features, making her breathtaking, but the pain lurking in the depths of those mesmerizing blue eyes caught him off guard, as much as seeing her at his family's table. She returned from his past, but Darcy introducing her as Jordan had given him a momentary pause. But the longer he stayed next to her, listening to the voice, his thigh rubbing hers, he knew this was his Lynn no matter what name she used.

But why the hell did he care?

She was the one who never called him after that night. And he'd be damned if he'd ask why or chase after a woman that didn't want him. Hadn't he been through enough?

Yet, here he was, reminiscing, feeling her, kissing her. *Damn it.* This black-haired beauty always carried a different affect on him. She made him feel alive, something he thought he'd never feel again. His body recharged, and the impact rammed him harder than the bullet that had pierced his shoulder.

She put her arms around herself in a protective gesture. "I was a teenager walking on the wild side. A little reckless if you ask me."

Where was this coming from? She'd trekked from wild and rebellious to borderline uptight. Was she capable of changing that much?

Yes. Look at April.

No!

He refused to venture down that road. After all, his ex-fiancée hadn't changed. His eyes just opened to her bipolar disorder. Never had he underwent this rush of adrenaline or gut clenching awareness with April.

Contrary to the words coming out of this lady's mouth, he refused to believe her. Sure, the girl in his arms had been out for a good time, a way to rebel against the rules her parents set, but she'd craved understanding of her actions. This he knew because she spent precious time explaining how people believed the worst about her, believed the boys at school. She confided how her reputation contained far more adventures than truth. How the tales were easier to go along with than deny.

And tonight, he caught a glimpse of that fiery female with one touch of their lips.

Trent crossed the room, noting the wariness on her face. He wondered how much more it'd take to break her ladylike demeanor and release her passion.

"Stop. Don't come any closer." Her pupils grew, and she shook her head, sending black hair sliding across her chest.

"Why?" He closed the distance. "Because you and I both know a lot more happened."

She'd confided that night how she enjoyed taking on the bad girl role, said it fed her spirit, and while she may have played around with a few guys, Trent was the only man she'd had sex with, save for one regretful first attempt. Not that he was proud of it, but knowing had stroked his ego. And starved for affection, for a tender hand, she gave every inch of herself over to his loving.

"You know nothing."

He put both hands on the counter, one on each side of her hips, and held her stare. "I know your parents conceiving you late in life embarrassed you 'cause your friends' parents were younger. I know your father's in a wheelchair, and at the age of seven you fell off your bike and broke your wrist. Then when you turned thirteen you became horse crazy. At fourteen you loved cowboys." He stepped closer, his chest grazing hers. "I know you lost your virginity to a heartless teenager who bordered from clumsy to an inexperienced ass. And you have a scar right here..." He ran a finger down to the tip of her right breast and fought back a smile when she sucked in a quick breath. "...from when you fell off a horse and landed on a jagged rock." He amazed himself with the details he recalled from her whispered words six years ago, and yet, he couldn't remember his ex-fiancée's birthday or favorite color.

Jordan's mouth opened then closed.

"I also know," he lowered his voice along with his head, "I drive you crazy when I kiss you here..."

Tasting the salty skin below her ear, he groaned and nipped her neck.

Her head fell back. "T-Trent. Stop. Why are you doing this to me?"

Why indeed? Taking one more nibble of her delectable flesh, he ended his attack and stared into the never ending depths of her eyes before catching her face in his hands. "I want to see sparks light up those baby blues."

"Please, leave me alone," she begged, shutting him out, but not before he glimpsed a flash of desire.

"I can't."

God, help him. His lips lingered above hers, and the suggestion of biting her bottom rim filtered into his head. The longing to rid the dark cloud hanging over her and release the spirit of the girl who'd stolen his breath flooded his senses.

She yanked free and vaulted away. "Why can't you leave it be? Leave *me* be?"

He'd been asking himself the same question since he brought her here, but those few hours they spent together were embedded in his memory stronger than any other. The girl he held in his arms was more woman than any he'd been with to date. She had a tough time growing up and hid beneath a tough exterior, but for reasons unknown, she let her guard down and opened up to him, telling him a lot more about herself with her body than words.

"Same reason you can't face me." He grasped her hips and pulled her vertebrae to his chest.

A small cry sounded from her lips.

"Life's about change. Sometimes not for the better, but you have to fight your way through," he whispered.

"I've faced my share of battles, and up 'til this mornin' I didn't realize how far I've let my scars take me."

He kissed the side of her neck and rotated her in his arms. Then, because the temptation was too great, he captured sweet lips in a passionate and frustrating kiss before walking out the door.

Chapter Five

Trent's mood spiraled downhill. Irritation ate at his gut. Confusion filled his head. Jordan showing up stirred many memories and feelings. Feelings he should have had for April. How, in the span of hours, could a person develop such a powerful bond with someone? One that drew him in with every fiber of his being.

He paced the grounds as guilt ate at him for having such a strong attraction toward Jordan.

April hadn't held his attention or his love. She'd been a body to hang out with, to argue with, to release physical energy. *Damn.* The admission made him sound like a calloused ass, but the need to acknowledge the truth for what it was filled him as he reflected on the night he met Lynn...Jordan. Like a magnetic force, an undeniable current pulled him to the raven-haired beauty from the first time he laid eyes on her dancing on the tailgate of his pickup.

She had been a wild, carefree, eighteen-year-old girl who stimulated him in ways he never fathomed. She had intrigued him from the moment her wide, blue eyes met his.

He leaned on the side of the barn and recalled the longing in her voice when she spoke of her life, how unfair things had been at home, and how her parents never understood. The sound of her sweet voice while she divulged the details of her past. The shy way she ducked her head when she realized all the information and feelings she confessed. How those blue eyes had gone molten when he sank into her warm flesh, and she arched her back and cried out his name.

Walking around to the front of one of the structures, he rubbed the back of his sweaty neck as images of her lying naked beneath him swirled in his mind's eye.

This line of thinking was only going to have him busting down her door, and that was not a good idea. Shaking off the memories, he entered the barn to check on Sierra. Having rescued her at a young age from an abusive home, the mare was his pride and joy. The horse stood quiet and solid, glancing at him as he invaded her sanctuary.

Placing his forearms on the ledge of the stall door, Trent watched the colt nurse. A new life, content, and at peace with the world. What did that feel like? Never having given his future much thought, he possessed no idea what he wanted out of life. His goals, much like his brothers', harbored around keeping the ranch strong and profitable. Though Nick's main focus shifted when he met Darcy, Sam and Chris's priorities stayed the same. But what about when they met someone?

Suddenly, the idea of keeping the same mundane pace for the next sixty or so years caused restlessness to edge along his spine. The ranch was his sanctuary, his...

Who the hell was he kidding? He wanted more. Wanted to be happy. Wanted...Jordan, and he'd be damned if he knew why.

Hearing the crunch of boots, he glanced over his shoulder.

Nick held out Trent's black Stetson. "Figured you'd miss this."

"Thanks." He took the hat and put it on his head before turning his attention back to the horses. "Looks like the little fella's fairing pretty well. There were times I wondered if we'd get this far."

"You've spent a lot of time with her." His brother thumped a thumb on the ledge of the stall, then turned to rest against the door, arms folded over his chest. "How 'bout you and Jordan?"

"That's none of your business." His family, the ever-meddling bunch. You'd think his brothers were a flock of hens since Darcy arrived on the ranch.

Sierra nudged his arm, and he reached out to rub her muzzle.

"Look, if it were up to me, I'd stay out of it and let you work out whatever mess you got your ass in, but Darcy's chomping at the bit. I had to 'bout hog tie her to keep her in the house."

That he'd like to see. "Sounds like your problem, not mine." He extracted a treat out of his pocket and fed the mare.

"Jordan's Darcy's best friend, and she's worried about her."

"Then go talk to her and leave me the hell alone." Irritated, he didn't bother to stop his voice from raising.

Nick smiled and rubbed his chin. "It's about time something lit a spark under your carcass."

"What the hell are you talkin' about?"

"You've moped around this place for two years, hardly smiling, never yelling. You talk in monotone and move with the speed of a snail."

"So."

"So, Jordan shows up and bam, you're alive. Cursing and yelling at me. Yanking her out the door." The eldest chuckled. "Must have been a shock to see her."

He was alive all right and scared spitless of the raw emotions rushing through him. Just the sound of her name caused his heart to pound. But he'd never confess such a thing to his brother.

"I can see why April felt threatened," his brother said in a low tone.

"It was one night." One damn night his girlfriend had thrown in his face for four long, hellish years— even though she hadn't technically been his girlfriend at that point.

He and April had split up a month prior to his neighbor's bonfire. Yet, she'd harassed him on a daily basis, followed him everywhere—even to that party, where she paraded around laughing in a drunken stupor, throwing wood on the fire, and pouring gasoline into the already blazing flame. He tried getting her under control and asked her to leave, which only led to a huge blow out before a friend finally took pity on him and escorted her home, or so he thought.

He'd been shocked when he found out she refused to leave that night and witnessed him and Jordan together. She'd watched them skinny dipping and enjoying each other. Boy, he caught hell for that incident. And being a sucker, he felt horrible for hurting her—even if unintentional—and somehow ended up back in the relationship with the monster. For years, he dealt with her emotional roller coaster, believing he was at fault, and she'd thrown that event in his face during every fight they had, which occurred daily.

Six years. Had it really been that long since he slept with Jordan? Hell, he could still feel her satiny skin, smell her sweet scent, hear the soft sounds she made as he tasted her body. All the memories April tried to tarnish. He shook his head.

Pushing off the stall, Trent started out of the barn and blinked at the night sky.

"You and Jordan definitely have the heat factor going on, I'll give you that. I waited for the smoke alarms to go off."

"Go to hell." He knew Nick pushed to get a rise out of him, but instead of retaliating, he hooked his thumbs in the front pockets of his jeans and sauntered toward the cabins.

"Maybe you should go for it, work off some of that tension."

Heat burned up his spine. What the hell had gotten into him? He had never known anyone in his family to be outright rude, but to insinuate he should use Jordan that way...

"Or did you piss her off enough that she won't let you back in her bed?"

Not able to hold back any longer, Trent lunged. "You son of a..." Hands fisted, he ran at Nick, taking him down. He swung, but missed when his brother veered to the right then left.

Although he made contact a time or two, the jerk did nothing but restrain him, albeit unsuccessfully.

"Is this what'll make you feel better? Fighting me? Hell, why didn't you say so? We could've done this months ago."

"Back off, Nick." He had no clue why he was mad, but the release felt damn good.

"I know what happened with you and April. I heard her tirades."

"Shut up." Lying flat on his back with Nick sitting on him, Trent pushed to dislodge the bulky meat-head but failed. His stupid shoulder refused to exert the strength.

"We *all* heard her outbursts."

Not able to free his hands and cover his ears, he shook his head, wanting to block out the words. God, he assumed they had witnessed the fights, but prayed he was wrong. The things that flew out of her mouth were embarrassing in themselves, some truths, some not. He wasn't sure which bothered him more, the lies or the details she revealed, usually intimate ones spouted in jealousy—how he paid attention to that other woman when she spoke, the way he touched her when they caressed, the way he held her in the pond. April had seen it all and made sure all of Amarillo heard her when she screamed the accusations. If she hadn't threatened to kill herself anytime he broke it off, begging him to understand how much she loved him until guilt ate at him and he gave in, he wouldn't have turned a blind eye to the problem for so long. Having his girlfriend live on the ranch when her apartment complex burned to the ground was the second biggest mistake he'd made—the first being the proposal. Every one of his relatives witnessed her temper-tantrums at one point or another. The fact she'd approached each member claiming Trent "ignored her" bore no help.

The recollection gave him enough fuel to struggle and manage to extract his hand out from under a leg and land one last punch to his brother's eye.

"Son of a…" Nick hit him in the jaw.

61

Stunned by the contact, he shook away the stars dancing in his head. "You jackass." He thrashed his body from one side to the other, but got nowhere.

Using all of his weight to hold him, his captor chuckled. "God, it's good to see you alive again, but are we done now? I'm getting to old for this shit."

Was he? *Yes. Damn it.* After all, he wasn't mad at the ox sitting on his chest. He was angry at himself for missing the signs with April, and for letting Lynn—Jordan—walk out of his life that morning.

"Yeah." He relaxed his body to prove his words. "Yeah, I'm good."

His opponent got up and extended a hand.

Accepting the assistance, Trent rose to his feet and rubbed his jaw as an uneasy feeling settled in his gut. That last night, when he came home after picking up a bull from Lubbock, April accused him of going to see a Jordan. Before he got a chance to ask who Jordan was, his fiancée drew a gun and shot him, twice. The next thing he remembered was waking up in the hospital groggy from surgery. He hadn't even known a Jordan, until now…was there a connection?

"It'll do you no good trying to figure April out," Nick stated, fingering the skin around his eye.

"I gave that up a long time ago." Wondering if his black-haired beauty was awake, he glanced at the first cabin. One small light shown in the window, but he couldn't make out any movement.

A hand touched his shoulder. "Put some ice on that." His brother nodded toward his face.

"You, too."

Trent shook his head and ambled off toward his own bungalow for what he figured would be a restless night's sleep. The past floated around his head, starting with a raven-haired beauty dancing in the moonlight.

****

Jordan tossed and turned until she fell into a fretful slumber. Memories circled in and out of her dreams...*Trent's lips on her neck, sliding down her body, biting her nipples, licking the beaded pebbles. His heart beating fast under her palm as she ran her hand up and over his chest, the thin, course hair ticking her skin.*

Her mother's face came into view. "Don't go out again. You just got home."

"Jordan Lynn!" her father bellowed out the living room window. "You better be home by midnight, young lady."

Then heat, scorching heat on her skin. Smoke choking her very breath.

Jordan shot up, coughing, and with a shaking hand, reached for the water next to her bed on the nightstand. The clock blinked bright in the darkened room. Four a.m.

Stretching out on the mattress, she concentrated on her breathing. In through her nose, out through her mouth. Her pulse beat loud in her ears. If she lay here long enough, maybe the anxiety in her chest would go away.

At five, she gave up and yanked on a pair of tan dress shorts with a thin fuchsia shirt. *Keep busy.* That was the next step. By seven, she paced the cabin. At eight, the walls closed in, and she slipped into a pair of brown flip flops and wandered outside.

The sounds of the ranch broke the silence screaming in her head. A cow mooed, answered by two more. The horses whinnied to each other, and the sheep rounded off the morning chatter. The golden dog ran, barking as it chased after one of the cowboys on horseback.

While the atmosphere was great for relaxing, if her days contained nothing but sitting around and watching the others work, she'd go mad. A person could relax for only so long. Maybe she should accept Darcy's job offer, but was that the wisest choice? Yes, the ranch was beautiful, and it would mean a paycheck…but it would also involve being in constant contact with Trent.

She walked over to the tree line and found an inviting path leading into the woods. Should she venture inside the unfamiliar forest? Certainly a walk would be better than the alternative of sitting here doing nothing. And if she did accept Darcy and Nick's offer, she'd have to familiarize herself with the layout of the land, so why not get a head start.

Not wanting to get lost, she kept to the trail, careful not to trip on any branches. Her shoe apparel provided little protection against the hazards of the root and twig carpet. As she roamed deeper into the forest, a calming silence wrapped her in a cocoon, and she wondered aimlessly down the aisle, glancing around for any wildlife. Exercise was definitely what she'd needed. Her heart felt light. No heaviness rested on her chest or shoulders. Serenity surrounded her, giving her a clear head to consider her options.

While taking the job would help her financial situation and boredom, dealing with Trent on a daily basis might be more than she could handle. And she refused to be naïve in thinking she'd be able to avoid him. The fact he lived here forced contact by its own violation, but was she capable of keeping the encounters to a minimum? Could she keep him at arm's length and…?

Ha. Who am I kidding? One touch of those sinful lips and she'd melt.

Heat from the sun beamed in through an opening of the trees, and she edged closer to a drop off. Birds chirped, flying high over a ravine. At the bottom, a creek ran the middle of the crevasse and opened into an oval pond. On the other side sat a rundown shack.

Gravity shifted under her feet, and Jordan grabbed the sapling next to her, hoping the tree spanned big enough to lend support. Was that the place she spent the night in Trent's arms?

No wonder she never found the hut. How had he driven to the site? Was there a road? A trail? She squinted in the bright light. A mosquito landed on her neck, another on her arm. Smacking at the blood suckers, she backed away.

Maybe Darcy knew a better way—she swatted another bug from her cheek—and knew where to get a bottle of insect repellant. Retracing her steps, she made her way back to the ranch.

"Hey, where'd you run off to?" Chris asked as he came from Nick's cabin.

"Just took a long walk." She bit her tongue to keep from asking him about the shack. What if the family didn't want anyone snooping around? Or worse, what if he insisted on going with her? She needed to do this alone. "Have you seen Darcy?"

He nodded. "She's working on the guest cabins. Come on, I'm headed that way."

"You sure it's okay to interrupt?" she asked, falling into step beside him.

"You kidding? We're pretty laid back around here, especially when there's not many guests, and knowing Darc, she'd love the break."

Glancing his way, she smiled. Chris made her feel comfortable. He had a relaxed way about him. He stood tall with a grin on his lips even when he wasn't looking in her direction.

"I hear you and Trent are old friends."

"A long time ago."

"He hasn't changed much." The youngest Matthews shrugged. "I mean, he's more guarded nowadays, but he's always kept to himself."

"Guarded how?" She tripped over a twig, and the cowboy grasped her elbow. "Thank you."

"Because of April. She did a real job on him. On all of us I guess." A dark shadow fell over his features.

Since he seemed to think she knew who this woman was and what she did to the Matthews family, Jordan refrained from asking questions. She'd save those for Darcy.

Looking ahead, she noted two men and a small boy hunkered down over an inanimate object in the corral. From the distance, she couldn't be sure, but it resembled the shape of a bull.

"How's it going?" Chris hollered to the trio.

"They'll be ready for the real deal in no time," Sam announced. "This kids a natural."

"I'll watch for his name in the next rodeo." Her tour guide waved and bent his head toward her. "That's Mr. Parker and his son. Sam's showing them how to rope. We use a fake bull so no one gets hurt. And that," he added as he nodded to the rounded woman and another boy standing nearby, "is his eight-months pregnant wife. She scheduled this trip last year, *before* she discovered her condition." He chuckled. "When she found out about the baby, she refused to cancel. Guess this vacation was a present for her husband. He always wanted to be a cowboy." He shrugged. "Anyway, here we are. Darcy's in one of them."

"Thanks."

"Any time." He hurried off in another direction.

"Hey, what are you doing out here?"

She pivoted as her friend exited the cabin with a bucket full of cleaning supplies. Her frayed jean shorts and gray top sported a couple of bleach stains, but a big smile lined her lips.

Someday she wished to emit as much happiness as her best friend. To feel a sense of rightness.

"Going crazy, but Chris was nice enough to show me where you were."

"Let me leave these in the other cabin for later, and we can head up to the main house for a coffee or cold drink."

"Coffee sounds excellent."

Darcy set the container inside the next bungalow and joined her with a scowl. The expression even looked out of place on her face.

"What's with the frown?"

"Where are the clothes you bought? Don't get me wrong, I love your outfits, and you always turn everyone's head, but I'd hate to see them get ruined." She groaned. "Now I sound like your mother, 'listen here young lady...'" She laughed.

"Ha. You're too funny. Don't worry, mother dear,

I'll be careful." Not wanting to explore the sudden emptiness in the bottom of her stomach, she changed the subject. "You want help cleaning?"

"A couple of hours ago I would've taken you up on your offer, but now, no. I'm almost done."

Climbing the stairs to the main house, Jordan held the door for her to enter. "I ah…went for a walk earlier."

"Good. I'm glad you're getting around and checking the place out." Her hostess crossed the kitchen to the coffee pot.

"The exercise felt wonderful. I came across a ravine with some sort of shed at the bottom. Do you know what it's used for?"

"The guys used to hang out there to get away from their parents and entertain their dates from what I understand." She quirked a lip. "Nick shared a few stories with me that I'd rather not repeat."

"Is there an access path or a trail leading to the base of the water?"

Darcy nodded. "If you walk a few minutes more on the path, there's an opening that winds down the hill." Standing on tiptoe, she grabbed two cups from the cupboard. "Nick took me once. The place is nothing but cobwebs." She poured the java into both mugs and handed one over. "We didn't stick around long. He said the structure wasn't sound. It's kind of creepy." Her brown gaze searched Jordan's with open curiosity. "You thinking of checking out the place?"

"Maybe."

"If you do, have one of the guys take you, okay?"

"I'll think about it," she replied, having no intention of asking anyone to accompany her.

Her friend studied her for a minute. "Jordie, what's going on? I get the feeling there's a lot I don't know. Especially about you and Trent. I mean, I don't want to pry, but I thought we were close, then I find out you two know each other, and your name was Lynn?"

Not sure how much she wanted to share at this point, she exhaled. "My middle name is Lynn, and truthfully, there's not much to tell. Trent and I spent the night at the shack when I met him six years ago. The next morning, we parted ways and never saw each other again." Knowing how it sounded, shame filled her chest as she glanced out the window to the empty drive.

"Six years ago? But you had to of been what…eighteen?"

Shrugging her shoulders, she didn't comment. Meeting a cowboy, giving him an alias, then sleeping with him, she'd lived up to every name the kids at school gave her.

A warm hand lightly touched her arm. "Let's sit out on the porch. It's a bit stuffy in here."

Following her out the door, Jordan sat on a chair by the railing. "You have to believe me, Darcy. I had no idea he was Nick's brother or I would've said something. I never knew his last name."

"I believe you, hon. And really, it's none of my business. I just care about you and don't like the stress I see all of this causing you."

Feeling as though she owed her friend, she went on. "When I first met Trent, I wasn't too sure of him, so I gave him my middle name. After we talked for a few hours and got to know each other, I never bothered to correct him. Seemed safer to keep it that way. He couldn't track me or tell my parents." Jordan shrugged, trying like hell to keep her voice strong and steady. The last thing she needed was for Darcy to suspect how deeply that night affected her.

A movement in the distance caught her attention as a horse and rider approached. A tingling traveled under her skin, and her heart beat tripled as the cowboy neared.

"You don't have to say anymore. I can tell you're uncomfortable, and the last thing I want is to cause you any distress over the situation."

With her back to the barns, the soon-to-be bride failed to see Trent.

"Hey, I know, why don't you grab a pair of jeans and go for a ride? Might help clear your head."

Her stomach fluttered with unwanted excitement. Another step toward the teenage years. She toyed with the idea of refusing while a part of her yearned to accept the offer.

"You can take my horse, TJ."

Oh, God, she really, really wanted to.

"Come on. Why do you beat yourself up over these decisions?" Darcy smiled as she inclined her head in a confused jester.

Too many situations propelled her closer to the past. The odds of slipping into her old ways stacked up. Still… "You're going with me, right?"

The cowboy reined his horse in at the base of the steps, and Jordan found she was hard pressed to tear her gaze away.

"I wish, but we have a big group coming in tomorrow, and I need to finish the chores. You can do a couple loops in the corral to get comfortable since it's been a while, and I'm sure one of the guys would show you around. That reminds me, it's Nick and my turn to take the guests on a two night camping trip. You wanna come along? It'll be fun."

"No. I'll be okay."

Listening with half an ear, she admired the way Trent swung his languid body out of the saddle. He tied the reins at the base of the railing and winked in her direction. She quickly pulled her gaze from the male who busted her staring.

"Are you sure? I feel bad leaving you—again. Never mind. I'm sure I can get one of the boys to take my place." Darcy sipped from her mug.

"I didn't come here to uproot your routine. I'll spend time at the hospital, getting reacquainted with the staff and making nice with the higher ups." So much for asking about April; she'd have to save those questions for another time.

The clunk of boots on the steps drew their attention.

"Hey, Darc." Trent tapped the brim of his Stetson. "Jordan."

Was it just her, or did his voice sound deeper, smoother, more throaty when he said her name? She met his hot stare. "Hello."

"Any left?" He nodded toward the coffee.

"You know Ms. Liz keeps it brewing." Darcy rose. "Let me get you a cup."

"I'll get it. Didn't mean to interrupt." Opening the screen, the hunky cowboy disappeared inside.

Looking straight ahead at nothing in particular, listening to the sounds coming from the kitchen, Jordan crossed one leg over the other and clasped her hands together around the cup. *If you act calm, you'll be calm,* she told herself. She glanced up, found a sad smile on her friend's face, and stood. "I took up enough of your time today. Besides, if I'm going to take you up on that ride, I should go change."

The door banged on the hinges.

"How's the shoulder?" Darcy asked, clearing her throat.

"Healing."

"Nice shiner you gave my fiancé by the way. Thanks." She scowled.

Trent rubbed his jaw line. "He had it coming."

Jordan sat back down as she noted a puffed up bruise on his chin. She caressed his face with her gaze, traveling over every inch, wondering what happened between the brothers. A gleam in his chocolate depths captivated her as a lazy grin lifted the side of his sexy mouth. She bit her bottom lip.

"You both need to grow up," his future sister-in-law huffed, folding her arms over her chest.

"What's the fun in that?" Trent chuckled. "Anyway, he sent me to grab those papers on the horses you discussed with Mom and Pop."

"I think they're in the office." She raised a brow in Jordan's direction. "Nick and Sam want to dedicate a couple of weekends throughout the year to holding special camp-outs for different organizations and groups, like Boy Scouts and Girl Scouts, even for handicapped kids. These horses are supposed to be as sound as they get."

"Let me know if you'd like help." She peeked over at the maddening male on her right, and a rush of heat ran the course of her body.

"I hoped you'd say that." Darcy faced her future

brother-in-law. "Jordan's a registered nurse."

"I've heard."

"Wouldn't it be great to have her on hand in case of an emergency?"

"Sure." His attention didn't waver.

After another quick eyebrow raise, she headed inside. "I'll...ah...go get those papers."

Sooner or later he'd have to look away, right? Jordan straightened in her seat and sipped the coffee to wet her parched throat, then made a project of wiping an imaginary spot off her shorts. The sun's rays caused perspiration to bead between her breasts. Shifting in her seat, she wondered how long they could sit in silence. Where the heck was Darcy? The documents couldn't be that hard to locate.

Trent drank more of his coffee and set the cup on the railing, never taking his gaze off her.

"Here ya go." The brunette returned and handed over the folder.

"Thanks." He snatched the file, tipped his hat back, and stalked over to stand in front of Jordan.

Her heart rate tripled, and her breathing became shallow as she gazed up the length of his never-ending body and over the hard contours his clothing outlined. A surge of desire ignited low in her belly.

Leaning down, his lips brushed hers, barely making contact, yet touching her too much.

Her toes curled against her sandals.

"I'll see you later." Angling his Stetson, he descended the stairs, remounted, and glanced up once more before heading toward the barn.

Oh, man. He was lethal.

Chapter Six

"Okay, well, today certainly turned into a scorcher," Darcy chortled. "Why don't you go change and meet me at the barn. I'll introduce you to TJ."

Jordan's legs refused to move. She didn't know if she was angry at Trent for the public display, or angry at herself for sitting there and letting him kiss her. How could the mere brush of his lips cause her to go all tingly everywhere?

A giggle caught her attention.

"It's either that or a cold shower."

A ride sounded much better than icy water. Besides, she could use time away from the tempting and distracting cowboy tying her insides in knots. "You talked me into it." Getting up with her empty mug, she crossed to the door.

"I'll take that. You go get ready." Her friend plucked the cup from her hand, and Trent's from the railing.

"Thank you."

Feeling the strain of the last few minutes in her chest, she drifted down the steps and headed toward the cabin, only to spot the troublesome man atop his horse. Not wanting to draw his attentions, she slowed her pace and hung back in the shadows.

Trent made an absolutely devastating, sexy image in the saddle, from the way he sat tall to the wide berth of his shoulders to the hat shadowing his handsome face. Her equilibrium tilted and dizziness washed over her.

A movement off to the side caught her attention, and she stopped in her tracks. The small boy she saw with the pregnant mom earlier snuck out from between the cabins and ran in the same direction as Trent. His feet traveling faster than his body, he stumbled, toppling over on to hands and knees. A cry broke through the air.

Instinctively, Jordan hurried to his side. "Are you okay, honey?"

The child struggled to right himself.

"Here, let me help you." She guided him to his feet.

Shrugging her off, he rose with tears streaming down his chubby freckled cheeks. Torn jeans revealed spots of red on the skin beneath. Eyes wide, he reeled toward the sound of a horse approaching and groaned.

"I'm okay." His bottom lip puffed out. "I'm tuff."

The envy on his little face as the rider neared tugged at her heart strings. "Let's bandage these up before you run off into the sunset?"

"Hey, partner, what happened?" Trent reined in his gelding and swung out of the saddle.

"Tripped over a stupid rock." He swiped the wetness off his cheeks.

Even the kid failed to be immune to the cowboy. The frustrating male bent on his hunches and inspected the damage.

"Don't look too bad, but best to let the nurse decide." He glanced up and smiled.

She stood motionless, observing the tenderness he

showed toward the child.

"Aw, I don't need no girl."

"All cowboys want a pretty lady to check them out." Standing up, the large man-child winked.

A sudden urge to kick dirt in his face propelled her over to the steps. "Bring the patient over to my porch, I'll be right back."

Walking into the living room, she struggled to compose herself. She'd tried over and over to envision Trent with children, but the images failed to materialize. Now, the picture was sure to replay a million times.

The rumble of the cowboy's low murmur floated in from the screen door and surrounded her in warmth. She closed her eyes and absorbed this new discovery.

"You wanna tell me what you're doing wondering off? Your mama's gonna be worried."

"Nah, she's gots the new baby coming to worry 'bout."

"Huh, I see. You think she don't care 'bout you anymore?"

Silence met the statement.

"Those mamas are amazing people. No matter what happens or what you do, they never stop loving you and have lots of room in their hearts."

"Really?" a small voice asked.

Jordan smiled at the question. She loved working with the kids at the hospital. They were so innocent and impressionable, and the highlight of her week when she'd been scheduled on the children's wing.

"Oh, yeah. When my younger brother was born, I was sure my parents would forget 'bout me."

"You're joshin'."

"Nope. One time, I even hid to see how long it'd take my ma to find me."

"How long'd it take?"

"Only a few minutes, but you know what?"

"What?"

"She cried really hard when she thought I was lost."

"Wow."

"Yep, and I never hid from her again. And believe me, your ma will always want you around."

"You sure 'bout this?"

"Cowboy's honor. Now…" Some shuffling noises sounded. "I wonder where that nurse is with those bandages. We have cowboy stuff to do."

Boots scraped on the porch as she hurried to the bathroom for the first aid kit.

"Jordan, you find what you need?"

"Right here." She met him in the doorway before he entered farther. "How's the patient?"

"Better," the boy announced from behind the impressive male body blocking the path.

Trent's gaze caressed her face, her chest, her legs, only to travel back up at an excruciating slow speed, causing heat along the path.

She raised a questioning brow, and he stepped aside for her to precede him out the door. Sitting next to the boy, she opened the lid and extracted a band-aid, ointment, and a cleansing solution.

"What's your name?" she asked, working the denim up over the injury.

"P-Peter." He glanced at Trent and squared his shoulders.

The brave front he faked for the adult male near

broke her heart. "How old are you?" Taking antiseptic, she dabbed his knees.

He squinted his eyes shut tight. "F-five."

Jordan blew on each scrape hoping to alleviate the sting before applying antibiotic cream and the protective pads.

"That should do it. You're an excellent patient." Patting her pocket she confessed, "Unfortunately, I don't have a lollipop."

"That's okay, ma'am."

She smiled at his politeness.

"You know what, partner? I keep a big stash of popsicles in my freezer. What's your favorite color?" Trent asked.

His face lit up. "Red."

"Mine, too. Be right back."

The urge to watch the cowboy wander over to his bungalow surged hard. She gazed to the right, down at her knees, to Peter on her left, anywhere but at the gorgeous backside disappearing inside the door.

"How long have you been on the ranch?" she asked the little redhead.

"Couple of days. Mr. Trent's real nice. He showed me the animals and even let me sit on his horse."

The admiration in his voice shouldn't have surprised her, but whenever she thought of *Mr. Trent,* he was naked in bed, not spending time with a five year old.

And he liked popsicles. Red ones to boot.

"You like horses?" she inquired as the distracting male headed back their way.

"Oh, yeah."

"Here ya go, partner." Stopping in front of the boy,

Trent handed over a frozen treat. "You eat that up, and I'll give ya a ride back to your ma on Rocket."

The boy's eyes widened. "You're really gonna give me a ride?"

He tipped his hat. "How else is a cowboy to travel?"

"Thank you," he replied and started in on the flavored ice.

"You sure? I mean what if his mom gets mad? Some parents might consider the animal dangerous."

The side of his lip tipped upward, and he nodded toward the guests' cabins. "I broached the subject of giving him rides yesterday with Mrs. Parker."

Conflicting emotions started. During the years, Jordan spent a lot of time building him into a carefree, irresponsible male out for a hot, wild time with no ties. She never imagined this warm, tender side.

Strike that. He'd been nothing but that with her. Yet, the way he responded to this child maimed her speechless as the gesture of his kindness worked through the tough shell she'd built around herself and wiggled its way into her heart.

Taking a deep breath, she stepped from the alluring scene to an oversized apple tree across the dirt path and wrapped her hand around a branch. The rough bark bit into her skin, offering a bit of realism as she gazed out at the animals dotting the pastures.

How much longer before Dr. Sheffield called? How much longer before she cracked? She glanced over to where Trent stood with Peter and caught him moving his shoulder in a slow circle. Was he doing too much? Not letting the surgery site heal?

As if sensing her gaze, his traveled her way; a slow

grin formed on his lips.

With a shake of her head, she turned away, focused on the land, and yawned, praying tonight the nightmares wouldn't come. Being close to this man, feeling his touches, his kisses, caused those taunting images to the surface all the more.

"Great tree for climbing." The baritone voice vibrated up her spine.

She spun around. The cowboy stood not two feet away, his black hat positioned low. The charcoal T-shirt hugged the dips and plains of his upper body to perfection, while the black jeans cupped lower muscles. Everything screamed sex…hot, sweaty sex.

Not good. Not good at all. Around him, her resolve weakened.

Guilt washed over her for her wayward thoughts, and she let go of the limb. "I'm too old for climbing."

"You might be, but I'm not." He ambled closer, his gaze not leaving her face.

"I'm younger than you." She stood stock-still, waiting, watching, unsure.

He brushed a strand of hair off her collar bone and rested a hand at the base. "Two years and five months."

She raised a brow in surprise. Her last boyfriend never remembered her age let alone the month she was born.

"Surprised?" he asked in a husky tone.

"Among other things."

A palm slid up the side of her heated neck as his thumb rubbed the skin along her jaw.

Jordan swallowed the moan working its way out. "Please, don't," she squeaked and backed up into the solidness of the tree trunk.

His arm dropped, but his brown gaze appeared watchful. "Why?"

Their gazes met and held.

"I'm not the same person. I've changed. I grew up."

"Haven't we all." He tugged his Stetson even lower and rotated his left shoulder.

"What happened?" she asked, nodding to his injury.

"What's with the dress clothes?" he countered.

"There's nothing wrong with my outfit." She riled, noting the way he avoided her question.

"And the Miss Priss attitude?"

"What, because I choose to dress nice I have an attitude?" The gall of the man.

He drifted closer; heat radiated from his body in waves. Her heart thudded in her ears.

"Every time I get close, you tense up. Why is that?" His gaze traveled up and down her body. "The girl I remember liked me close, *real* close and would've opted to wear jeans on a ranch. Not that you don't look amazin', 'cause darlin', you're hot no matter what you wear." He leaned into her. "Or don't wear."

Her body tingled, and she licked her dry lips. Oh, why couldn't she muster up the strength to push him away?

His gaze dropped to her mouth. His finger traced her bottom rim, then with a wink, he turned away as Peter walked over to them.

"Mr. Trent, I'm done."

Not missing a beat, he hunkered down in front of the child with a chuckle. "We should clean you up before we go see your ma." A dark, hungry gaze swung her way. "We'll catch up later."

Not if she could make herself scarce.

The pair strutted away, and Jordan was hard-pressed to ignore his retreating backside. He wouldn't find her later; going for a nice long ride would keep her out of his reach.

Dang it, she'd lost track of the time and forgot to meet Darcy at the barn. Fishing her cell out of her pocket, she dialed her friend's number.

"Hello," came the breathless answer.

"I'm sorry. I got delayed," she explained, biting her lip to keep from babbling.

"That's okay, hon, but I needed to get back to work." A loud bang sounded.

"You, okay?" she asked, worried over the background noises.

"Sure, just dropped the bucket, that's all. TJ's brushed and ready to go. Chris is waiting for you."

"He's going with me?" Jordan swallowed her alarm and hoped Darcy didn't hear the distress in her voice. She really needed this time alone.

"No. He has chores to do, but said he'd watch you do a few laps in the round pen to make sure you and TJ get along. He was saddling the horse when I left."

"Thank you. You're a gem." Hitting the end button, she crossed to the cabin as Trent and Peter walked out of his bungalow.

He lifted the child onto the saddle and a grimace of pain crossed his face. She started toward him, but as she approached, he mounted behind the boy and winked in her direction before trotting off.

****

Trent went the long way to the cabin where the

Parker family stayed in order to give the boy a longer ride. He tried focusing on Peter's excited jibber, but his mind betrayed him by straying to Jordan. Back by the tree, he lost track of everything and was lucky the little guy interrupted or he would have kissed her senseless.

His hands tightened on the reins. Something didn't sit right about her. The dress clothes and suit of armor confused him, as did the challenge in her eyes. She seemed so tense, like a rubber band ready to snap. *Maybe that's who she was,* an inner voice whispered. Lord knew he wasn't an expert on her after one night together. Hell, if his track record stood correct, he wasn't an expert on a woman after years together.

But Jordan tried hard to come across as cold and uptight, yet didn't stick her nose in the air at him or his family, even treated Darcy with the love of a true friend. And the longing when she laid those baby blues on him, the hot, unheeded passion in her kisses, and the way she dealt with the boy when he fell...the caring and compassion showed a contradiction to what she tried to portray. And a total opposite to the way his ex handled things.

To April, kids spanned from messy to an irritating nuisance. If she'd spotted the accident, she'd have ignored the child and stomped off the other way.

Matter of fact, she had made Trent deal with the smaller quests on the ranch, claiming the whiny brats gave her a headache. Why had he wasted a hay wagon full of time with a person he bore nothing in common?

"Mr. Trent?"

"What's up buddy?" he asked, shaking off the unwanted memories.

"If you tell my ma you took me for a ride, I won't

have to tell her I ran off without permission and followed you?"

Chuckling at Peter's logic, he paused long enough for the kid to believe he considered the explanation. "I'll make ya a deal, if you promise not to wonder off again, I might be inclined to say I saw you outside and offered a ride."

"Oh, you *are* kind, Mr. Trent."

"What's that?" Not sure what the boy rambled on about, he bent forward.

"You said you'd be kind to tell her."

Trent bit back his laugh. "*Inclined.* It means willing to go along with your plan." He stopped his horse, dismounted, and helped his passenger out of the saddle as Mrs. Parker came out the front door.

"Peter John, where have you been? I was worried sick." She hurried over and hugged her son. "I'm sorry, Mr. Matthews. My husband and older boy went off with one of your brothers, and since Peter was playing, I decided to lie down for a few seconds. I must've been more tired than I thought." She rubbed her protruding belly. "This one tends to zap the energy right out of me."

"I can imagine." Not really, but she sure had her hands full with Peter and the baby to come. "He was no trouble. Matter of fact, I asked him to go with me. Figured it'd be okay since Mr. Parker let him ride with me the other day."

"Oh, yes. I trust you. My cousin, Trish, lives up this way. She knows your mama and speaks very highly of ya'll."

"Mr. Trent gave me a popsicle," the child broke into the conversation.

"Cherry flavored, I'm guessing."

"How'd you know?" He frowned in confusion.

"Moms know everything," she told the boy, wiping off his red mustache with her thumb.

"Then how come you didn't knows where I was?"

Trent smiled and dug into his pocket. "Here's my cell number. If you need a break or someone to watch this cowboy, give me a holler. If I can, I'll take him for a while."

"Oh, no. I couldn't."

"Yes, you can." He tucked his card into her hand. "And you"—he knelt down—"listen to your momma."

Standing, he caught sight of another horse heading toward the woods. From the slender shape on the animal's back, he figured the rider to be female—the very woman who wiped the cobwebs from his soul and kicked his heart rate up.

Chapter Seven

As TJ started toward the path to the shack, Jordan's stomach heaved. This wasn't her best idea. Maybe she should leave the past where it belonged, in the past.

Nonsense.

She wasn't going to find out anything of significance. The memories those walls held were already stacked up and bundled for sorting. What the person discovered depended on who searched the details. For her, it was the place of being cherished and loved. A place she needed to see one last time.

Jordan scanned the area as the gelding picked his pace down the ravine until the creek bed remained the final obstacle. The ripple of the current flowed in a gentle race into the mouth of the pond on her right. Large oaks and overgrown brush lined the area, breaking way to reveal a dirt road big enough for a vehicle. The same one Trent used to drive to the enclosure? It had to be. If she closed her eyes, she could feel the truck bouncing over the uneven ground, then jerking to a stop inches away from the creek.

She had laid down next to him in the bed of his pickup to watch the stars. Being relaxed and intoxicated on him, she hadn't needed the two beers to loosen her tongue. She told him all about her parents, her horse, her dreams, her fears, anything and everything that had been her life.

Jordan could still feel the sensation of his knuckles on her skin as they skimmed the side of her cheek. How his calloused thumb had felt as it trailed over her lips.

She squirmed in the saddle as she recalled those intimate moments when she had nipped the tip of his finger with her teeth. He pulled her body over his and asked her to show him how she rode her horse. Throwing caution to the wind, she straddled his waist. Surprised by the feel of his erection pressed hard against her center, she rocked her hips. He thrust upwards, to imitate the way a horse would buck her off, then he flipped her over and had taken complete control.

"More run down than ya remember?"

The deep Texas accent startled Jordan and caused goose pimples on her arms. She swiveled in the saddle. Trent's warm gaze made contact, and the breath suspended in her lungs.

"I don't think anyone comes here anymore." He leaned a tanned forearm on the pummel.

Inhaling deep, she straightened, shook off the nostalgia, and gave the horse a slight nudge. TJ trotted across the shallow river, stopping inches from the shack.

"You going inside?" His horse splashed through the water, stopping next to her mount.

"No." At least not with him.

The side of his mouth lifted in a seductive way that melted her resistance.

"Scared?"

"Of what?"

Not breaking eye contact, he swung out of the saddle, strutted over, and grabbed her horse's reins.

She dismounted, careful to keep her body from touching his.

"The memories," he answered, his face inches from hers.

Turning away, she closed out the images and sent up a silent prayer for strength to deal with the tempting cowboy. Her heart pounded as she watched the water travel over the rocks downstream. She'd wanted to make this trip alone, to face the demons by herself. How could she sort through the pain with the man at the core of it all right next her?

"Come on, I'll go in with you."

She pivoted to find he had secured the animals to a nearby hitching post and now stood at the door. Stiffening her back, she charged over to the entrance.

"Ladies first." Mr. Manners held the wooden barrier open.

What sounded like a smart idea earlier now gave the distinct feeling of walking straight into the lion's den.

Doing her best not to brush against the massive chest filling the narrow doorway, she crossed the threshold and traveled back in time. The cabin appeared exactly the way Darcy described it, and nothing like Jordan remembered. Cobwebs hung from the ceiling in the corner. Dust covered every inch of the small space. Tracing a finger over the wooden paneling, she winced when the grit came off on her skin. She bent and wiped the dirt off on the edge of a folded gray blanket at the foot of the double bed, on the mattress that held many secrets.

The sinfully, delightful things Trent did to her body swirled in her mind. Her gaze rose to his. The heat she encountered caused a shiver of awareness to race down her spine.

Not breaking eye contact, he set his hat on a dust covered, makeshift table.

Jordan took several deep breaths and turned her attention to the room. Wouldn't take too much to clean the place up, couple of rags, disinfectant, a mop. She walked around, stopping when she did a full circle. Damn, but the space was small, especially with a large cowboy standing in the center, watching her every move.

A warm hand grasped her arm, turning her.

"Don't."

"Why?"

Gritting her teeth, she studied the wall over his shoulder, the fabric of his dark shirt, anything but the depths of the knowing brown orbs. Damn him, and the affect he held over her. She shut her eyes and stood straighter, then called on every ounce of strength she possessed to reject him. She would not let her guard down. She would not give in to temptation. She would not—

Soft lips nuzzled her forehead, and she swallowed the whimper that rose inside as he tugged her closer.

Step back. She needed distance, but her feet inched forward. The heat from his body felt good.

You aren't a teenager any more. You're a grown woman. But being in his embrace was as shockingly stimulating as she remembered, and she was caught between heaven and hell, between the memories and the desires.

His arms tightened, making any argument next to impossible. What was wrong with her? Her brain turned to mush, and the flashbacks gained free access. Memories of his lovemaking, their talks, more lovemaking, that feeling of belonging and contentment, of someone understanding and listening to her weakened her resolve all the more.

Then came the flames…the smoke…the smell…

Trent gazed at the woman curling into his chest as if she couldn't get close enough. Her body tensed, and he felt a tremor run through her; a slight shiver he may have missed had they not been standing completely still. As much as his ego wanted to believe he could affect her that much and the reaction was pure physical pleasure, he suspected otherwise.

"You all right?"

"Yes."

He raised her head. Worried now over the paleness of her skin, he placed a palm on her slender shoulder. "Sit."

The bedding wasn't the cleanest, but beat the alternative of having her land on the floor if she passed out, which he figured was highly likely by her ashen color.

Taking a seat beside her, he seized her hand. "Jesus, your fingers are like ice." The air wasn't cold in the cabin or outside. He rubbed her skin, trying to warm the digits.

"I'll be okay. Give me a minute," she mumbled, staring straight ahead, inhaling and exhaling slowly.

Damn. A trip down memory lane shouldn't cause her to go into shock. Grabbing the blanket at the end of the mattress, he rose, shook the dust off outside, then wrapped the cotton around her shoulders. "Look at me."

She shook her head, refusing to show him those

baby blues, something he very much wanted—needed—to see. He grasped her chin and tilted her face upward.

Jordan's eyes shut, but not before anguish and pain flashed in the endless depths.

"Let me rest a minute." She extricated herself and reclined on the bed.

"Why?" he asked baffled. "What's going on?"

She rolled over facing the wall.

"Damn it, what's with you? Is it that hard for you to let me in?" Silence met his ears. "Are you sick? Answer me?" What the hell did he get himself into now? When he followed her to the cabin, he figured they'd share a few memories, a kiss or two, and hell, who knew what else. When they were together, he lost all common sense.

"I just need a minute." She took several more slow, steady breaths.

He placed a hand on her side. Her body quivered beneath his palm. Not sure what was happening, he was torn between staying and going for help.

Unable to desert her, he stretched out behind Jordan and rubbed her back, hoping to have a warming effect. "Talk to me."

After a few minutes she sighed. "I told you about my parents?" she asked.

"You told me they're older than your friends' parents. Your dad's in a wheelchair because of an injury from a war, and your mom spends most of her days caring for him." He grinned, recalling her words. "They're strict and unfair and don't understand anything, especially yo—"

"They died the night I was with you."

Shocked over her whispered words, Trent wrapped his arm around her middle. "Damn. I'm sorry, sweetheart." Unable to imagine losing his own parents, he kissed the crown of her head. "Why didn't you call me?"

"I couldn't find the number you gave me." She sighed. "Six years later, and the day feels like yesterday," she mumbled. "I was so immature, always complaining about them when all they were trying to do was protect me."

He rose on an elbow and shifted her until she lay face up. The distress in her features tore at his heart. "Darlin'," he began, caressing her, "that's a long time to be carrying around this guilt."

She sat up and clambered over him.

"Jordan?" He grasped her arm, but she shoved him away and began pacing the room.

"You don't understand. It's more than that. My parents are dead because of *me*."

He reared back and blinked several times. "What?" Had he heard her correctly?

"I went home to a pile of ashes. Our house burned to the ground. My parents couldn't get out." Crossing her arms, she stared out the window.

"How's that your fault?" He stood, grasped her small but solid biceps, and spun her around.

"I should've been there. I could've helped. I'd have gotten them out. They'd be alive today if I hadn't…" She sniffed, but tears failed to fall. "The fire chief's report said it appeared my dad's wheelchair tipped, and my mom couldn't get him back in before a beam from the ceiling fell, trapping them."

"You honestly believe you're to blame?"

Astounded by her logic, he tightened the hold and refused to let go.

"Yes." She tugged away.

His heart ached. How could he get through to her? Had anyone tried? He didn't think so, if years later she continued to take such blame. How different would his own mishap have turned out if his family abandoned him during those rough days? His family...the very ones he continued to give a hard time.

"You're not," he whispered, kissing her cheek.

"I could've saved them if I'd stayed home, if I grew up to be the respectable young lady my mom prayed for...if I hadn't missed curfew that night."

"Most teenagers don't listen to their parents. I didn't."

"But I cost mine their lives."

"Jordan." Taking her head in his hands, he brought her inches from his face. "That's crazy. What could you've done?"

"Gotten them out."

"Or *died* tryin'." The words sliced through him, and his throat muscles constricted. He wanted to shake sense into her, make her listen to reason, alleviate the distress.

"I—"

"Don't say it." He pulled her into his arms.

"My parents needed me, and I let them down." Her breath slid across his skin as she tucked her face into the crook of his neck. "I always disappointed them."

She didn't say it in hysterics or for attention. Her words were quiet, but spoken in a strong manner, which worried him all the more. Had he traded one unstable woman for another? Distrust fisted inside him.

No. He refused to believe that.

"Lord, help me," he whispered.

That wasn't right either.

Lord, help the female I hold in my arms.

And *there* was the difference. With April, the need to get away when she carried on consumed him. With Jordan, the craving to stay surged strong. She didn't break down in tears as he suspected, but the pain on her face showed real emotion. The anguish evident in every feature. He possessed an uncontrollable urge to correct her way of thinking, to aid as her crutch, as his family aided him.

Her head raised and honest blue eyes shot straight to his soul. She withdrew and fled toward the door. "I'm sorry. I didn't mean to fall apart. I really should be going."

"Jordan." He stepped across the small space and stood in front of the exit.

"You think I'm a whack job. I see the accusations in your eyes."

"No." He squeezed her hand, praying for the right words.

"I'm usually able to keep my emotions in check and keep the anxiety to a minimum."

"Anxiety, huh?" Now that was a condition he knew about. Although his symptoms were slightly different, he recalled the heaviness in his chest, the uncontrollable shaking. He spent countless days and nights consumed by the demons. His brother, Sam, witnessed the first attack and helped him deal with the hell—later, medication aided him.

"You need to let go."

"I have let go. I've cried. I—" She yanked away,

but he held fast.

"Is that why you parade around in those fancy clothes, afraid to laugh or get close to anyone?" He shifted, fighting the urge to rub his shoulder. The brawl with Nick definitely hadn't helped the damn ligaments. "Why are you punishing yourself?"

She twisted one more time, then stood still, staring him in the eye. "My reasons may seem ridiculous to you, but my mother always dressed nice. She hated when I wore jeans. She was a bit old fashion and said men wore denim, not women…"

"So, to honor her memory, you banned the clothes from your wardrobe?" The whole situation seemed preposterous, but he saw real hurt lurking in the shadows of her gaze. She truly believed everything she told him. Over the years, she let remorse and guilt weave their way in until, little by little, the emotions ate away at every aspect of her life. "Is that why you hold yourself back from people, not letting anyone see the real you? Because you're afraid of who you are?"

"I don't. I'm not. Look at Darcy and I…" She folded her arms across her chest. "We're close. She knows me."

"That's why she knew nothing about us?" The tip of his thumb swept across her soft lips. "Come on, darlin', I see the shame in your eyes. I feel your pain. I hear your words before you speak." He may not have been sappy with April, but he was certainly making a jackass out of himself right now and sounded like a sappy love song. What worried him more was the fact he didn't care.

"Not possible."

Trent cupped her chin and kissed her—hard,

driving out any doubt forming in her beautiful head. If someone told him a week ago, or even yesterday, he'd be this aware, this connected to another person, he'd have accused them of being crazy. Yet, he hadn't felt this alive in a long, long time. Six years to be exact, when he'd last held her.

"Have you talked to anyone 'bout your parents' death or the fire?"

"I'm an RN. You think I'd get away with no counseling."

"You tell me, 'cause no one seems to have corrected your way of thinking."

"There's nothing to correct."

He peered into her eyes, willing her to see the truth through him. "You *aren't* to blame. You weren't home. You were a normal teenager, rebellious and young. Why can't you see that?"

Her gaze held his as if she wanted to believe him, then she shut him out. "It's getting late. I should head back."

Wrapping her stiff body in his arms, he kissed the sweet skin on her neck. "Have supper with me," he murmured.

She shook her head, and stared at the floor. "Thanks, but I've humiliated myself enough for one night."

He nipped her earlobe. "Please. We can ride back together. I'll take care of the horses, grab food from the main house, and bring it back to your cabin. That should give you enough time to shower and cook up more arguments for me."

Chapter Eight

Two hours later, Jordan sat, picking at the meal. Inner turmoil swept her up like a tornado. Years of perfecting her life, perfecting *herself*, bordered on being for nothing in Trent's presence. These past years, she'd been walking around numb, incapable of loving anyone, or being loved. The man wore her down. That and the fact she liked the feelings he evoked...liked *feeling* period.

Shifting in her seat, she stabbed the fried chicken. "This smells delicious."

Was he right? Would her parents still have perished if she'd been home? Would she have died trying to rescue them?

Plenty of people had suggested the same, but it was his words circling her mind, his voice she heard, his woodsy scent invading her sense of smell, his love... No. He never uttered the strong word.

Setting the dish on the coffee table, her hand closed around the cold, wet glass of water.

"Tastes even better." He frowned with a nod toward the untouched plate.

"I'm really not that hungry." Because fear ate at her gut, leaving behind a pile of rocks.

Telling him about her parents was hard, but the real problem lay with the secret she still harbored. Maybe once she got that off her chest the anxiety would ebb to a minimum. He deserved to know, but would the information matter? The outcome remained the same. Would he want to know? Would he even care?

The syllables ran around her brain, but failed to make the journey past her lips. If she didn't say what weighed on her mind, her conscience was sure to eat her alive. Worrying over how he'd react, she gnawed on her bottom lip.

"I can hear you thinking." He set the half-eaten food next to hers. "What's up?"

Mentally requiring space, she stood. Maybe she should just blurt it out and let him decide what to do with the information. Blurting probably wasn't the most ladylike way of dealing with the situation.

"I told you what happen when I arrived home…but not everything." The knot of nerves fisted tighter in the base of her stomach, and she twisted her fingers together. "I caused my mom and dad a lot of grief…"

Trent lifted a hand, growling as he stood. "I'm here to listen all you need me to, and I may not have known your parents, but I'm sure they'd want you to be happy." He rotated his left arm. "Do you think mine were pleased with everything I did?"

Watching him work the limb, she ignored reasoning and trudged on. "After the fire, I lived with my aunt. She told me my mom prayed and prayed I'd turn out okay. She cried because of me." The daily sermon hovered around Jordan's selfishness and what her shenanigans cost everyone, what her bad judgment cost the whole family.

"Sounds like a great aunt," he mumbled.

Jordan lifted her gaze to his. "My relatives are very religious, and I'm the sinner of the bunch." She looked down at the floor. "The black sheep."

Strong hands grasped her arms, not quite digging in, but enough to grab her attention.

"Look at me, damn it."

She couldn't. "You don't understand."

Trent gave a small shake. "What warped sense of faith did your aunt believe in? Families stick together in times of tragedy, not blame one another. I should know. I've tried my parents' patience plenty, not to mention my brothers'." He slipped a strand of hair behind her ear. "We were young adults having fun, and enjoying each other in the process." His lips teased her in a quick, sensual kiss. "End of story." Thumbs rubbed back and forth, causing a ripple of heat to the surface. "You need to let this go and forgive yourself."

Her hands landed on his chest to put a few inches between them, but got caught up in soft fabric molding the muscular plains. "I tried for weeks to find the cabin, to find you..." She searched his face for reassurance and the strength to continue.

"The bonfire was at Charlie's, our neighbor on the main route. His access road leads to our woods. That's the way I drove you to the shack." Warm hands dropped away, leaving emptiness behind.

Taking in the tilt of his head, the tenderness of his gaze, the way he smiled that sexy half-grin, renewed every second of the past. Renewed her faith in him.

Stay on track. Focus. The words swirled on her tongue. Instinct told her to trust him, and holding on to that glimmer of hope, she plunged on.

"After that night, I changed my ways. I signed up for college like my parents wanted, I stopped partying..." She rambled, but couldn't stop the flow.

"…but it was all too late. My parents were still gone. I had no idea how to reach you. I wanted to find you, to tell you—"

He seized a hold of her, clenching his jaw. "I know, but you have to stop beating yourself up over this. Tomorrow, maybe you should go talk to someone. I'll go with you if you want, but this can't continue."

Realizing he thought she was talking about her parents again, tears burned behind her eyes, and she fisted her hands, digging fingernails into her palms. "I stopped drinking and took care of myself. I don't know what went wrong. The doctor said the situation couldn't be helped. I'm sorry, Trent, I…I lost your baby. She was stillborn."

Trent reeled back and stared in disbelief. Had she just said *baby*? *His* baby?

As the impact of her statement sank and settled heavy in his chest, he inhaled a shallow breath, feeling as though he'd been punched in the gut. This wasn't about her parents anymore. This was about Jordan and him. And a baby. Jordan carried *his* baby. She gave birth to *his* baby. Was that even possible? Of course, they made love, but he used a condom every time—in the back of his pickup, in the cab of the truck, the shack, and…the pond.

The pond. She dove in to cool off, things got heated, and…

Having a hard time wrapping his brain around the concept, or what any of the information meant, he needed to hold on to something solid and threaded his fingers into the silky strands of raven black hair as his lips brushed across her forehead. His body sidled toward her, seeking some sort of contact without any conscience thought. The warmth from her body heated his.

"And yes, I'm sure you're the father, because you're the only man I've been with, other than my first time."

He froze. The admission stunned him, and this time he stepped back. How could that be? "No one else?" he asked, surprised at the rawness of his own voice. This was all too much to take in.

"No."

"You mean even since…"

"No." She grabbed his shirt front in her fists, her gaze on his. "I have never had sex with anyone other than you, okay. There. Happy now?"

"Never? Not in the past six years?"

She had to be lying. No one went that long without—

"No."

He sucked in much needed oxygen. "Damn, darlin', you really know how to knock a guy out of the saddle." He rubbed a hand down his face, taking a second to absorb it all. How was it possible this woman only had sex with him? How was any of this possible? Too many thoughts tumbled into his head to sort. Too many denials. No way could this be true. How…? Why…? Only him? She only slept with him…

The fact no other man had touched Jordan since, and the very idea of her having carried his child crippled him.

"Please don't hate me. My aunt told me it was God's way of punishing me. That I was a sinner and deserved what happened."

As shocked as he was, the plea gripped him like a

vice around his chest. Though this would take him a while to grasp, none of it was her fault no matter what she believed.

"Your aunt needs her head examined." He'd love to call the woman and give her the name of a few shrinks. Maybe take a side trip and beat the hell out of the ex Darcy talked about. Then again, he should thank the guy. Because of him, Jordan came back to Texas. Had she really not had sex with the live-in boyfriend? He shook his head in an attempt to collect his thoughts.

The baby. He needed details. "What happen with the baby?"

She rested her forehead on his chest for a minute, then her gaze rose to his as her palm pressed against his heart. "Labor was long, and right before entering the birth canal, she rolled and came out breach. The doctor tried to help, but…she died from asphyxia, a lack of oxygen."

The words tumbled out with a dry eye, and other than a slight crack in her voice, were void of emotion. During all the confessions, not one tear fell, but she couldn't hide the tremor that shook her body or the slight quake of her hands.

Trent imagined she cried plenty over the years. She was strong, brave, and honest. To overcome such heartache by herself and come out on top proved a true testament to her strength. These little breakdowns caused, no doubt, by months, years of listening to the all-holy aunt, but he planned to undo the manipulation the witch instilled.

"Darcy didn't know about the baby?"

"No."

Needing something solid under him, he sat on the

sofa. As if the strength left her body, she sank down beside him, and he stifled a groan as his shoulder thwacked the back of the couch. The nuisance stiffened more and more. A lot of truths were coming out tonight, and as much as the truth pained him, he admitted the doctor may have been right. His non-compliance prolonged the healing of the injury. But he'd worry about that later.

"When are you going to tell me what happen? I mean, what led up to rotator cuff surgery?"

Not able to shift gears so quick, he mumbled, "Hazards of being a cowboy."

"Uh-huh. Somehow I doubt that."

Not wanting to discuss any part of the past involving April, he went back to the matter at hand. "You said, *she*?"

"Yes. We had a baby girl." She pushed herself from the couch. "I'll be right back."

Even as boggled as his brain was, he still admired the graceful way she sashayed out of the room. How should he act when she returned? Should he question her? Doubt her? She gained nothing by claiming to have given birth to his child...his daughter.

Wow, talk about a stampede stopper. The whole turn of events felt foreign, and his mind spun.

"Here." She reentered the room and handed him an envelope. "I could never bring myself to throw them away." Raising a slender shoulder, she continued, "They were taken about three weeks before she was born."

Wondering if he should break the seal, Trent flipped the paper over in his hand.

"I think it'll end some of your disbelief."

He slid the seam open. Slipping two fingers inside the fold, he extracted a couple of black and white photos, and his Adam's apple lodged in his throat. Although he was able to make out almost every detail, he still asked, "What exactly am I looking at?" He glanced from the image in his hand to the woman beside him. Cold fingers clutched his forearm.

"They're sonograms of our daughter. It's amazing how far they've come and how much detail they're able to pick up." Her gaze cast downward. "She looked almost identical when she was born." A sad smile framed her lips.

Covering his hand with her own, longing crossed her beautiful face, and he knew then and there he'd give her the world if he could.

"I'd give her the moon."

Nick's words echoed in his head, robbing him of speech. He swallowed the emotions and inspected the next picture. Although taken at a different angle, the photo didn't look much different from the first.

"You can't tell by these, but she had the same birthmark as you." She shrugged. "Guess that's something else you'll have to take my word for."

Jordan had traced the outline on his thigh a night long ago, telling him the shape reminded her of a horseshoe. As a young boy, he accused his parents of branding him and his brothers with the symbol, but found only he and his father sported the mark.

He rubbed a thumb over the image. His mother still had ultrasounds of his brothers and him, but none this graphic.

The very concept of this woman having his child inflicted a strange protectiveness to fill his chest. She swore to having his baby, yet only the single proof remained, two black and white pieces of film. The infant died during birth, therefore none of this mattered. But the idea of a baby…

He needed air, time to think. "I have to go."

Trent stood and placed the photos back in the envelope. Slim, cold fingers wrapped around his.

"Take them with you."

The confusion he suffered reflected in her expression, making him feel like a heel for rushing off, but the mass of tangled barbed wire in his brain required straightening without distraction.

"Thanks." He stared into her open, honest features. "We'll talk more tomorrow."

She nodded, and he kissed her forehead. His lips lingered on the soft skin. Her body trembled, and he felt even more of an ass. She needed reassurance and understanding, but the words were struck in his throat. Placing his Stetson on his head, he headed out the door.

Chapter Nine

Trent rubbed his chest as an ache settled in the center. Disbelief and uncertainty over the information he discovered filled him.

The facts Jordan presented didn't change his future or hers, but if the baby lived, that would've been a different story. He'd have a daughter to care for, a start of a family. One without April. No way would he have exposed his baby girl to that bitch of a woman who hated children. His life would've evolved into something entirely different if his daughter had survived. If…

The pain Jordan must have suffered carrying a life inside her only to have the infant ripped away in the end unmanned him. No one should have to endure that kind of heartache.

The circumstances following their night together ended in tragedies for both of them, but more so for her. Yet, she managed to get through the trauma and proceed with her life, coming out on top. A true testament to her character and the woman she'd become.

And here he sported a grudge over not being one hundred percent, refusing to listen to his family or the doctors in order for the injury to heal. Instead, he drove himself to prove he needed no one, while she retained not one person in her corner.

What a bastard he'd been.

Swinging open the barn door, he stormed to the back room where his father had hung a punching bag decades ago. He laid the precious envelop on the shelf with care, then slammed his fist into the object hanging from the ceiling. Chains creaked against the rafters as the sack sailed across the small room.

Adrenaline pumped in his veins as he swung at the bag repeatedly, feeling a slight release of the tension in his muscles. His shoulder burned like hell, and he soon found himself drenched with sweat.

Jordan would have been a great mother. Wasn't fair the baby died. Continuing to pummel the bag, he beat out his anger and frustrations over the past, the pain suffered at the hands of others, at the hands of chance, and because there was not one damn thing he could do to change the outcome. That's what bothered him most. He wanted to help her; to make things better for her as his family had him, to explore the unexplained connection he felt toward her. And how could he forget the intimacy factor. She went up in flames any time he kissed her, turning into a wanton woman. Her response alone swelled his ego.

"That thing owe you money or steal your girl?" Sam caught the object as it sped toward him.

Ignoring the comment, Trent bent over, hands on thighs, to catch his breath. Every time he turned around, one or more person from his family were there, waiting for him to need them.

Because they care, he reminded himself.

"I don't think this is the kind of therapy your doctor prescribed."

Straightening, he met his brother's watchful gaze.

"Right now, it's the kind I need."

A brow dipped over one eye. "I'd think the fight with Nick would've cured that." Sam crossed the room until he stood boot to boot with Trent. "Damn it, kid, don't you get it? We're all tired of watching you wallow in self-pity. Don't you think two years is long enough to let April win? You think you're the only one in this world who's had rough times? You know what, you wanna be pissed off the rest of your life, go for it."

Unsure how to take his brother's outburst, Trent confiscated the envelope on the shelf. "You're right."

"And don't give me some bullshit about…what'd you say?"

"You're right." Seeing his hat on the floor, he placed the Stetson on his head, and headed out of the room.

His brother fell into step beside him. "That was too easy, and you're the least agreeable person I know. What gives?"

While he didn't relish the idea of announcing the news to the entire clan, telling one member of the herd was a start. He handed over the packet.

His older sibling raised a brow in question as he examined the contents and stopped walking. His confusion gave way to a frown.

"Is that a baby?" Sam turned the picture different ways, then glanced from Trent to the picture and back. "You telling me you're gonna be a daddy?"

The impact of the words took his breath once again. The idea of Jordan carrying his baby scared the hell out of him, but knowing there was no baby only mildly overcame the initial fright. Now his chest just ached. He rubbed the spot in the center.

"Who's the mother?" he asked, sliding one photo behind the other.

Trent pointed to the top where Jordan's name was imbedded into the film.

"*Jordan?* How? When?"

He lifted a hand to silence the questions. "Those were taken eight months after Charlie's graduation bonfire."

"Cripes, that was six years ago. Where's the baby now? I didn't see a kid with her. Are you sure it's yours?"

A couple of horses ran in the pasture, catching his attention. With no easy way to explain, he looked back at his brother and blurted, "She was stillborn."

Sam's mouth opened and shut several times. "Damn. That's a hard one to swallow."

"Tell me 'bout it." He rubbed the nape of his neck to ease the building tension.

"These pictures—"

"Are sonograms taken three weeks before she delivered."

"Talk about a major blow." Sam shook his head.

"Yep." Unable to stay still any longer, he stuffed his hands into his front pockets and strutted off in the direction of the cabins.

"What now?"

"Damned if I know." He walked along side his brother, feeling his support and worry hanging heavy in the silence as the pair made their way across the land. Support Jordan never had.

"You going up to the main house for supper? Ms. Liz stored leftovers in the fridge."

Trent glanced over to where the rest of the family

would surely be, and for the first time, noticed dusk had fallen. "I already ate." Getting close to the house, he stopped walking.

"From what I can see, this doesn't alter your life." Sam handed back the images.

"Feels like it should." His mom and dad raised their boys to be polite, use their manners, and own up to their responsibilities, but he wasn't sure where that fit in with this scenario. He kicked a rock in the path with his boot and continued forward.

"Definitely gives you two a connection, but one you're not obligated to continue, or, if you decide, to explore." His brother turned and headed up the stairs to the porch.

He mulled over Sam's last comment as he entered his cabin minutes later. Truth of the matter was, the more he entertained the thought, the more he liked the idea of being a dad, which shocked the hell out of him. Who was he kidding? The situation vanished before he even knew the position existed.

Heading to the shower, he stripped, and stepped under the hot spray, hoping to clear his head. An hour later, restlessness fisted in his gut, chasing him from bed. Tugging on his jeans, he hobbled out to the porch and stared up at the starlit sky. How'd life get so mixed up? Before Jordan returned, he was...

Nowhere.

His life was idle. Not moving forward, stuck in the routine of daily life.

Where did he want his future to go? What did the next sixty-some years hold?

Land for sure. Hell, he'd never give up ranching, but the idea of being alone for the rest of his life held no appeal. Sure, his brothers were here, but someday they'd have spouses and new lives. Nick already started.

Did he want to follow in big brother's footsteps?

Trent glanced around and found a light shining in Jordan's living room window. Without pausing for thought, he ambled over the pebbled ground and knocked on the door.

The woman he needed to see appeared on the other side of the screen. Her hair was swept back from her freshly scrubbed face, and she now wore a navy blue tank top with gray, cotton shorts.

"Did you forget something?" her soft voice asked as she clutched the door, her gaze glued to his chest.

"Can I come in?"

Without a word, the barrier opened farther.

Jordan wasn't sure what to think when Trent entered and stood in the center of her living room, shirtless. When he deserted her earlier, she figured he'd keep his distance…far away.

"I want to apologize for cutting out."

Insides quaking with nerves, she tore her gaze from the rising and falling muscles of his upper body.

"Thing is, I'm not sure what to feel, or what I'm supposed to feel." He ran a hand through his hair.

"You don't have to feel anything. Nothing's changed." For him anyway. Angry with herself for the bitterness, she gritted her teeth to keep the words in.

"Everything's changed, but I'd be damned if I can explain why." He sighed and closed the distance. "There's something 'bout you."

A large hand slipped to her neck. Instant heat bolted down her spine, and she stifled a moan.

"I feel more around you than I have anyone." The sexy cowboy rested his forehead on hers. "For the record, I'd have been honored to be our little girl's d-daddy," he whispered.

A mountain of chills ran over her body.

Was the testament so easy for him to say because the situation no longer existed?

Tender lips played with Jordan's, causing her knees to weaken.

"And you'd have been an awesome mother."

Rather than sink into the strong, masculine pull, she held back, afraid to believe, afraid to give into temptation.

"I want you." He nuzzled the side of her throat. "I need you. You're like the missing half of me, and that scares the hell out of me."

She wanted him, too, but struggled with the decision to give in.

Tell him to go before it's too late.

Tipping her head, she got caught in the web of his gaze. Her tummy tightened and fluttered, sending a tingling sensation to every nerve ending. Her resolve weakening, she leaned into him. How good would it feel to let herself go? To feel alive and not like she walked around in someone else's body.

Trent cupped her cheek in his calloused palm and wrapped the other arm around her waist, drawing their bodies closer together.

A tidal wave of sensations flooded her senses at the feel of him. His tongue traced her lower lip, and before she drew another breath, his mouth crushed hers.

An adrenaline rush like no other traveled through her. Her hand flattened against his chest. Skin to skin.

This was wrong, yet right.

Frantic for more, she launched her own assault, kissing his lips, jaw, chin, neck, and back to his sinful mouth. It had been so long. *Too* long. Tracing a path up the hard contours to his silky hair, an ache pooled heavily at her core.

High on his scent, dizziness washed over her. Her mother always told her to keep her head out of the clouds. What was she doing? This was wrong. She owed her parents the courtesy and respect she failed to show them during those high school years.

No. Jordan rolled the thoughts aside. *I'm an adult now.*

His hand slid underneath the hem of her shirt, skirting her ribs, and up to cup her breasts. The feel of his palms through the thin cotton covering her nipples was her undoing. She needed this. Needed *him*.

Leaping up, she wrapped her legs around his waist.

He caught her and cupped her backside, squeezing, kneading as he carried her to the bedroom and placed her on the mattress.

Trent paused next to the bed, giving her a minute to study his well-sculptured muscles. She licked her dry lips. His torso—though broader than she remembered—sported a thin layer of dark hair in the center and two scars. One she assumed resulted from his surgery, but the other was farther down, below his rib cage. What happened to cause such angry lines? She reached out and touched the puckered skin.

Strong hands closed around her upper arms. "No."

She jumped and searched his face, noting an underlining uneasiness. Rising on her knees, she kissed the surgical spot.

He tensed under her administrations, but didn't stop her.

She nibbled her way up to his neck and collar bone and back down the magnificent chest, tracing his nipples with the tip of her tongue. Licking the salty skin across his flat abdomen to the waistband of his jeans, she made quick work of the belt buckle blocking her way. She was stunned by her own brazen actions, but unable to calm the hormones raging inside her malnourished libido.

A shudder ran through him before he trundled her back on the mattress and kicked free of the denim. Her gaze filled with narrow hips and dark blue boxer briefs. She reached out to trace a fingernail over the erection concealed in the underwear and over to the birthmark on his left thigh. Once, she thought the symbol odd and intriguing. Now, the horseshoe held heartache and love, nightmares and memories.

"My turn."

The sound of his deep drawl and feel of hot hands on her skin yanked her back to the present.

Trent slipped her shorts down her legs and drew the tank top overhead, exposing her lace-covered breasts and skimpy black thong.

"I see you still like sexy underclothes." He wrapped his arms around her and pressed his mouth to the exposed mounds of skin above her bra. She arched to meet wet lips and shivered as his kisses traveled down to her rib cage.

The magic, the sizzle she remembered was real.

Heightened sensations caused her to thrust into the impressive bulge growing behind the cowboy's briefs.

"In a hurry, are you?" He released the front clasp,

freeing her to his waiting tongue, and flicked the pebbled nipples one by one.

Ultra sensitive to his administrations, she grasped the back of his head and held him tight as she had before. This was how he made her feel all those years ago. A few touches and she went up in flames. The chemistry between them hadn't diminished by any means.

"Please, Trent."

He suckled harder, sending waves of wet heat rushing to her center, dampening the thin material of her thong.

She grabbed his hand. "You're driving me crazy."

"Can't have that now, can we? Tell me what you want," he murmured against her skin.

She placed his hand at the juncture of her thighs. "Touch me."

He grazed her breasts with his teeth as he cupped her, slipping a finger in and out of the side of the silky barrier.

Jordan gasped at the rush of overwhelming sensations. She was on fire, and he had only begun to stroke the coals.

"I can feel your heat. You're so wet."

In one fluent yank, he ripped the lace off, and replaced his hand with his mouth.

She sucked in a breath as his tongue flicked over the sensitive area.

"You taste so good." He stroked her in and out, up one side, down the other, and back in.

No other man had ever made her this hot, this crazy, this wild. Abandoning all her reservations, she let herself go completely to the only person she'd ever trusted. Her hips moved, meeting each thrust harder, faster, her orgasm building. Light exploded behind her lids, and she called out his name.

His body slid back up, and she opened her eyes to stare at the most desirable male she'd ever met. Her heart fluttered and skipped a beat as Trent's sinful mouth met hers.

Needing to explore him as he had her, she shoved at his upper body until he sprawled back on the bed. Once again, she was drawn to the scar close to his shoulder and the one on his lower abdomen. Wanting to savor the moment, and save anymore talk for later, she lavished each as if she could kiss the marks away.

She explored him with her hands, fingertips, and tongue, reacquainting herself with the taste and feel of him. Licking at the salty skin and kissing her way across his chest, over his torso, and lower. Catching his gaze, she pulled the briefs away and grasped his shaft. Slowly, she slid her tongue up the thick length and over the rim, remembering the way he liked her to those many years ago.

His penis twitched in her palm as she wrapped fingers around the velvety skin. Watching him watch her, she took him into her mouth and sucked hard. Not once, but twice she glided her hand up and down.

"Stop." Trent dragged in ragged breaths. "No more."

Flipping her onto her back, he leaned over and opened a drawer on the side table.

"What are you doing?"

He let out an audible sigh and revealed a small packet. "Praying these were still here."

"How'd you know they were?" Thankful the

package was there, she wondered where the prophylactics had come from in the first place. Had he brought other girls to the cabin?

Of course he'd been with other women. She'd be stupid to think otherwise. A bit miffed with the idea, but trying not to be, she gave a quick laugh.

He grinned from ear to ear.

"What?"

"You're jealous."

"Ha! Of what?"

"You think these are mine. That I've had sex with other women here. I see it in your eyes."

Damn. How could the man read her so well?

Trent cupped her chin in his palm and smiled. "Darcy used to live here, and Nick mentioned…well never mind. Just know they aren't mine, but lucky for us, there's a box left."

He leaned down, and warm lips touched hers. Feeling like an idiot, but more at ease and happy with his explanation, Jordan snagged the condom from his fingertips, ripped the foil open, and rolled the rubber down his length.

"Time for a ride, cowboy." She shoved him playfully onto his back and slid a leg over his waist, eager to feel him.

Large hands grasped her hips, holding her suspended over him. He pushed upward barely touching her opening with the tip of his penis.

She wiggled. "Trent, please."

Slowly, he lowered her onto his awaiting shaft. Her breath hitched at the invasion. Savoring the feel of him deep inside, she closed her eyes. The sensations so long waiting, so long in coming.

"You're tight," he hissed through gritted teeth and cupped her breasts, kneading the tissue.

Her body stretched, accommodating his thick size. She lifted up, and sank back down, burying him deep and rocking against him. He fit so perfectly, felt so good. Tipping her head back, she pressed her breasts forward.

He bit a nipple with his teeth and suckled one then the other, before holding her face in his hands and bringing her lips down to his.

She nipped at him and pulled back, staring into his brown eyes. Only with this man had she ever let her guard down or felt cherished, and she wanted, for the first time in years, to embrace herself and what may be in her future.

Believing in herself and the man who held her heart, she released her fears and lowered the walls she'd built to protect herself.

"God, you're beautiful." He thrusted upward, driving harder, deeper, faster.

She leaned forward, scraping her nipples along his chest, and bit at his jaw. Sure hands slid around, cupping her ass, spreading her open. She bit her lip to keep from crying out his name at the erotic sensations.

His finger slid between their bodies, and his thumb circled her sensitive nub. She wanted the pleasure to last, but the pressure was too intense. Every nerve ending screamed out. Powerless to stop wave after wave, her heart thudded in her ears. The orgasm flowed more intense than the first and she gasped, hearing him shout her name as he, too, let go.

Chapter Ten

Jordan rubbed the sleep from her eyes and stretched. Her aching body protested the movements, and she smiled, recalling the reasons.

A heavy arm landed across her midsection. She shifted closer and planted a kiss on the cowboy's lips.

"Mornin'," he murmured, brushing strands of hair off her shoulder.

He ran the finger over her collarbone, up the side of her neck, setting fire with every inch. For too many years, she longed to be close to another human being...well, not just anyone. She never found this heightened place or sense of security with any other than Trent.

She glanced to the clock on the bedside table and blinked to clear her sights. No way. Sitting up, she exclaimed, "I can't remember the last time I slept past five."

Trent half-rose. "What time is it?"

"Seven," she answered, staring into his handsome face.

A hand shot through his hair, causing the strands to stand up on end. "Damn. I need to go. I should've been at the barns hours ago." He rose and picked up his pants off the floor.

Watching him draw the denim up his naked thighs, she wished for another hour or two to lie in bed with

119

him, keeping reality at bay for a while longer.

"You okay? You got a funny look on your face."

"What? Oh, I'm fine." She tugged the sheet up over her breasts.

The mattress dipped with his weight as he sat. His finger traveled along the ridge of the cotton and dipped into her cleavage, his tongue soon following.

Goose pimples rose on her skin, and she closed her eyelids, savoring the feeling.

He moaned and crept over her, forcing her to lie back. "I guess a few more minutes won't matter."

And who was she to argue when his mouth inflicted such delicious assaults.

Hands grasped her hips and flipped her over; his fingers and lips traveled down her spine, setting the skin on fire. He kissed every inch of her back, biting her ass lightly until she withered against the sheets.

"Lift up." Wrapping an arm around her waist, he positioned her on to her knees and slid a finger over her vagina once, twice.

A heaviness settled low between her thighs, and she pushed back toward the sweet torment of his errant finger, wanting more. He inserted another, slipping in and out, shallow then deeper, slow then faster until she thought she'd go mad.

Jordan whimpered as she tried to hold back her climax. She wanted to feel him throbbing inside, to feel his thick size stretching her, pleasuring her when she went over the edge.

He pulled out and pushed back in at a rapid pace, bringing her orgasm that much closer, but withdrew at the last second.

"You are so cruel." She turned to see what he was

doing, but a strong arm held her still.

"Don't move."

He reached past her and grabbed a condom, then spread her legs farther and mounted her from behind. The invasion sent a shock to her core. Never had she imagined feeling so wanton. He withdrew and plunged inside again and again, his testicles slapping against her sensitive flesh.

His fingers traveled up her back, gently pressing the top half of her onto the mattress, while his other snaked around to find her swollen nub.

"Oh, I'm..." She bit the pillow, pushing back, wanting him deeper, harder, faster. Stars danced behind her eyes as he moaned her name, and she tumbled over the ecstasy cliff with him.

An hour later, he rose. "I really need to get out of here or my brothers will hunt me down." Kissing her lips, he stared. "Go for a ride with me later?"

She giggled. "We already did."

"Horseback riding, you nymph." He bit her neck. "I'll swing by in a couple of hours."

"Okay." She smiled, reveling in the happiness and contentment that filled her.

One more quick brush of his mouth and out the door he went.

Jordan shook her head and marveled over the changes one day could make in a person's life. Sinking back in bed, she inhaled Trent's lingering scent on the pillow. Maybe she'd stay right here until he returned.

****

After a quick wash and shave, Trent headed to the barns, whistling along the way. His mind at peace, his muscles relaxed for the first time in years. Being with

Jordan last night—and again this morning—was hot, sweaty, intense, and...like coming home after a long, hard rodeo.

"I see you finally decided to show up," Sam commented, walking out of the horse barn.

"Didn't mean to stick ya'll with the chores."

His brother scrutinized him with open curiosity. No doubt wondering if he swallowed more pills.

"Don't worry, we saved the best for last. Chris is in the cattle barn, and that leaves you, my friend, with the small animals."

"No problem." Nothing could sour his mood. Feeling like ribbing his brother a bit, he asked, "Why is it you were the one who brought pigs, sheep, and smaller critters to the barn, but we seem to be the ones cleaning up after them?"

"Because I'm brilliant, and they're a rip roaring success with the guests, especially the children. Hell, they even provide some food for the business." Sam chuckled, swinging a bag off a skid and loading the feed into a storage bin. "Missed you at the meeting."

"I'm sure ya'll did fine without me." He started off, wanting to get his duties done and hurry back to Jordan.

"That permanent smile you're wearing wouldn't have anything to do with a certain dark-haired woman staying in Darcy's old cabin, would it?"

Trent refused to comment as he continued toward the pigs, whistling.

"When you get done with the small barns, you were elected to give the grounds a once over," his sibling yelled out, stopping him in his tracks.

What the hell!

"That'll take most the day," he complained,

retracing his steps.

Sam shrugged. "No one checked the fences last week, Chris is helping Mr. Parker with another lesson, and I have to run into town to tie up loose ends before I head to Tulsa."

"Weren't you just in Tulsa?"

"Just check the fence. Darcy and Nick'll be leaving for camp today. They can check the back lines."

He noted the way his sibling avoided the question, but let him slide. Sam's comings and goings were none of his business. Besides, he wanted to hurry things along and get to the main attraction.

Maybe Jordan would want to ride fence since they were going out anyhow. Might be a good time to talk and find out more of what she's been doing over the last six years. She never did say what started the fire that killed her parents or how she came to a be nurse.

Finishing the pens in record time, he hurried to throw a lunch together, saddled the horses, and secured a lead rope to pony her mount with his. He headed her way, feeling like a teenager going out on his first date, and a little foolish at the same time. The woman affected him stronger than any other, and that scared the daylights out of him. There was something about Jordan that wrapped around him, a protectiveness toward her, the need to love her and help her, to be her anchor. Yep, he definitely lost his mind...heart and soul.

Trent reined the horses to stop as he approached the cabin and Jordan stepped outside. Blue jeans molded every delectable curve, moving with her like a second skin. A white tank top clung to her upper half, sculpting her breast and revealing enough cleavage to leave him drooling.

"Is this horse for me?" she asked, coming closer.

"Yes, ma'am." He dismounted, and in one swift movement, pinned her between the animal and his body.

She laughed and tilted her head back, bringing her luscious lips inches from his. Feeling like a starving man, he lowered his mouth and devoured her. She tasted of mint and smelled like sunshine. Blood rushed to his southern hemisphere, leaving him dizzy with want. He pushed his growing erection into her, leaving no doubt how much he wanted her.

Petite hands crawled up his chest, to his neck, and played with the hair on the back of his head. He loved the feel of those delicate fingers on his skin, especially when they traveled below his navel.

A searing heat rushed clean through him. Needing no more encouragement, he pivoted and walked her backward toward the cabin until she broke away.

"Aren't we going riding," she panted.

"We are." He just decided on a different kind. "But we need lots of practice first."

"Trent." She put a palm between them, holding him at bay.

"Jordan," he growled, moving forward as she stepped backward.

Lifting her hair off her neck, she fanned the skin with the other hand. "I want to see the land. We have all night for...other things." She smiled with a devilish glint and secured her thick main at the base with a tie she had on her wrist.

Knowing she was right, he ran a hand down his face. This wasn't the time. Work first then play. And boy, did he plan on playing…hard.

"Let's go, woman. We don't have all day." He stepped toward her mount, anxious to get going so they could get back.

Jordan giggled and shook her head. "I can get in the saddle by myself."

"You sure, darlin'? 'Cause if I let you struggle, it wouldn't be very gentlemanly." He gave her an appreciative once over.

"And if you help me, we'll never leave." She put her foot in the stirrup and swung her leg over the rump.

"I reckon you're right." He mounted and looked her way to be sure all was right.

"This isn't TJ?" She stroked the side of the Appaloosa's neck.

"No. Darcy's taking her horse on the camping trip. You're riding Champ, and this is Lucifer."

She laughed. "Of course."

Loving the sound of her enjoyment, he smiled and asked, "What's that suppose to mean?"

"Wouldn't expect the big bad cowboy's mount to have any other name." She giggled again.

"For your information, this happens to be Sam's. He hasn't been out in a while and needed the exercise." He pouted, pretending to be wounded by her words. "But I forgive you."

"Thank you for small favors." Her eyes danced with amusement. "Where're we headed?"

"I was hoping you'd accompany me while I check the fence lines, then we can stop for a bite to eat in the south pasture." He patted the bag behind him.

"Sounds like fun."

Fun for her, hard for him as he watched her body

rock in motion with the horse.

They traveled in silence for the first few minutes, and he noted her taking in the surroundings. He tried to look at the property with an unbiased eye, and a sense of pride filled him. No matter what happened in his life, he could always count on this, on the serenity of the land.

"Did your parents live on farms when they were children?" Her soft voice floated over him.

"My dad, but not mom. Although this"—he swept a hand out in front of him—"was her dream."

"He didn't want the ranch?"

She squinted in the bright sun, and he kicked himself for not reminding her to wear a hat.

"He loves this place, but loved my mom more, and thought she'd want a house in the suburbs with a white picket fence and all the trimmings. When he inherited the property from my grandparents, she confessed her dream of having a dude ranch. He wasn't sold on the idea right off, but she has a way of getting people to see things her way. After a few years of raising cattle and horses, The Matthews Dude Ranch was born."

Jordan's sweet laughter filled the air. "Sorry. I don't mean to be rude. It's just from what I saw of Tammy at the hospital, she's a force of her own."

"You've met my mom?" This was news to him.

"Mm-hm. Twice when she came in with your father for his tests."

Strange how he wondered about this woman over the years, and here the people around him encountered her a time or two. "You know the details of my dad's medical problems?"

"Just what Darcy told me."

"Then you're aware of his condition?"

"Some, yes."

"To hear my ma tell it, you'd think he had a major heart attack instead of a few warning signs."

"It's her way of taking control of the situation. I'm sure hearing the man she loves has cardiac issues scared her, but sounds like they caught the problem before anything too serious happened. Is he exercising regularly?"

"I believe so. He complains when they're home about the work outs he has to endure during their trips."

As they reached the crest of a hill, he moved his horse closer to the fence line and dismounted once to check a sagging section.

"Do you like having a dude ranch?"

"Truthfully, I'd rather tend cattle or train horses, but it pays the bills."

"What about your brothers?"

"Nick and Chris are okay with things the way they are, but I get the feeling Sam would rather raise livestock. He's the reason there's so many. For a while there, he brought in strays every day."

"Strays?"

"That's what my brothers and I call all the small animals as a joke." Reaching a flattening in the land, he asked, "Feel like stopping to eat?"

"Don't we need to check the rest of the fence?"

"Nick and Darcy'll check the back side during the camping trip, and we can scope out the rest on our way back."

"Then yes, I'd love to eat." She followed him to a tree and dismounted. "Is the entire property fenced?"

"No. We keep the animals close. The rest of the

land's woods and wild life." Trent secured the horses to a branch in the shade before digging through his saddle bag for the sandwiches and the water he packed. How stupid of him. He never asked what she liked.

"Hope cold cuts are okay?" He wheeled around. Jordan stood a few feet away, staring out over the open space.

Eyes a tinge darker than the sky faced him. "Not much I don't like in the way of food." She smiled and sat in the grass as he handed over the main course.

Peering down, he kicked himself again. "Guess I didn't plan this very well."

"What do you mean? This is great."

"I should've brought a blanket."

"This is perfect." She placed a corner of the sandwich in her mouth and chewed.

Damn. Just the sight of her eating shouldn't turn him on.

"This is very good. Ever think of becoming a chef?"

He laughed at her attempt to make him feel better. "Throwing a few pieces of meat between two pieces of bread doesn't qualify for any culinary awards I'm afraid."

Setting his hat on the ground, he nodded and settled down beside her. He bit into his own food and stared out over the terrain. On the ride up, he shared more of his life with her than he had with anyone. Hell, he probably talked more than he had in the last five years. If he could only get her to reciprocate and share a bit about herself and what's been going on, but he had a feeling it would take some probing on his part.

"What made you decide to become a nurse?"

"A family friend mentioned it a couple times when I was in high school. My mom and dad loved the idea." She frowned. "Of course, I wanted nothing to do with anything they approved of so I never took the career seriously." She stared out straight ahead. "When my parents died and I had no idea what to do, Dr. Sheffield, he was my father's closest friend, sat down with me and discussed my future." Her slender shoulders rose. "At first, I think I agreed with becoming an RN because my parents wanted me to, but now, I really do love what I do."

"From what little I've seen of your skills with Peter, I think you made the right choice."

Leaning back, she raised a bottle of water to her lips and guzzled a dose before catching his eye. She was just as beautiful now as six years ago. Time had not aged her, but he did note a little harder of a shell she kept around herself. How could she be single after all this time? The men she encountered had to be blind.

Jumping in feet first, he asked, "Am I really the only man you've had sex with since? I'm not questioning the baby factor," he hurried to explain, "just seems odd you slept with a virtual stranger and not a guy who lived with you."

She coughed, apparently choking on her sandwich, and grabbed her water, drinking more liquid. "How'd you know about him," she asked, lowering the bottle.

"Darcy spoke of her friend moving in with some jackass." He shrugged. "I just didn't know you were *the friend*."

Jordan had analyzed the same question over the years, and stared straight ahead as she gave him the only conclusion she had come to, "The one boy I was with before you tarnished a very innocent night, twisting the evening into tales of orgies. He and his friends turned the details into a hell of a lot more than the truth. The rumors flew from me being with one guy to a gang bang with the whole damn football team." Even though she revealed a few of the details to him six years ago, embarrassment flooded her. Oh, how she detested high school.

Mustering up courage, she stole a glance his way. Except for the slight dip of his mouth and white knuckle hold on the rim of his hat, he displayed no reaction.

"I guess as a stranger, you held no perceived judgments about me. In a bizarre way, I felt safe sleeping with you, free to be me and let my guard down."

A smirk lifted one side of his lips. "Bizarre, huh? Much obliged for that." He chuckled, then sobered. "So, what 'bout the guy you lived with in Nashville or Kentucky or wherever the hell you shacked up?"

Jordan smiled. "That's part of the reason he left me. Seems he wanted a woman who'd do more than lay next to him in bed." She bit another piece of the sandwich as an awkward silence filled the air. Why couldn't she keep her mouth shut?

Trent shifted closer. "You have a little something right here." He leaned forward and nibbled the corner of her mouth.

Loving the feel of his lips on hers, she made a pitiful attempt to wipe the spot away with a finger. "Where?"

"Here." His fingers slid into her hair as his breath caressed her face.

She drew back and licked her lower lip. "That line is over used."

Trent's gaze shot to the motion of her tongue and a flicker of heat ignited in his eyes. "I'm okay with not talking at all."

He pulled her to him and kissed her with a potent combination of care and passion, his lips hot and compelling on hers. Jordan whimpered and snuggled closer. After their night together, how could she want him so badly? Yet, there was no denying the desire rising deep within. She was crazy about this man, no matter what happened in the past. She loved that he was strong and capable, yet tender and caring, and the gentle way he handled Peter pushed the wall she erected around herself down a few more inches.

A palm slid over her side to her behind, cupped her back end, and squeezed.

"Damn, you feel good."

Oh, God, so did he.

He kissed her with unhurried tenderness, making her feel cherished, like a porcelain doll that may break with the slightest pressure. Her body warmed and a throb deep inside drove her closer. She threw a leg over his and pressed against his muscular thigh. Winding her arms around his neck, she lost herself in the feel of his strength, the heat of his body.

Trent moved his hands back up to cradle her face as he pulled back, breathing hard. He rested his forehead on hers and stared into her eyes. "We should head back."

Chapter Eleven

Jordan's knees wobbled to the point she wasn't sure how she'd managed to get back in the saddle, but here she sat on Champ, following Trent back to the barns. The man turned her on with one touch, yet walked away as though nothing happened. The bulge in his pants told her he was turned on, but she worried he didn't feel the same. Maybe his was just a physical reaction.

"I have a question."

His deep voice broke into her thoughts as he slowed his mount, bringing them side by side.

Fearing what was to come out of his mouth, but having nothing to lose, she masked her hurt with a smile and glanced his way.

"What caused the fire at your parents' house?"

Without hesitation she blurted, "Arson." The word hung in the balance as she waited for him to say something.

"They catch the person responsible?"

"Nope." Waiting for his judgment of her bore too much, too painful, and she nudged her horse to a trot.

"Jordan." He caught up in a split second. "I didn't mean to trudge up bad memories. You never said, and I wondered."

"They accused *me*, okay!" she shouted and slowed Champ.

Trent's hand snaked out and grabbed the reins, halting the horse. "What?"

Under his watchful gaze, she squirmed. "Rachelle, the girl I drove with that night, left the party without me, and I couldn't prove where I'd been. They concluded I killed my parents." The pain of the accusations sliced her like a knife, plain as the day she was hauled downtown and placed in an interrogation room.

She grasped the lines connected to the horse's bridle and tugged, wanting more than anything to run away from the memory. "Can we go now?"

"Just like that, huh? Subject closed?" His grip tightened on the leather.

"Yes." Tears burned in the back of her eyes, but she refused to let them fall. That part of her life happened so long ago, but at moments like this it felt like it was happening now.

"And here I thought we were getting to know one another better. I opened up to you."

"Opened up? Is that what this afternoon was about?" Jordan laughed in his face and shook her head. How could he possibly believe he opened up to her? "You spoke of your family, your family's land, your family's animals, your dad's medical problems, but not one fact about Trent. Nothing about your shoulder, or…" *Who April is*, she added silently. "Nothing. Oh, wait, you did tell me you wanted to raise cattle and train horses. My mistake." He had a long way to go if he thought that was sharing. He wanted facts, fine she'd give them to him. "You want the dirty secrets of my life? Here ya go…I mourned my parents' deaths while being accused of their murder. I spent hours surrounded by police officers and detectives, being questioned and having to reveal every second of those twenty-four hours. Telling virtual strangers how I spent the night in some cowboy's arms and in his bed when I didn't even know his last name. To make matters worse, I couldn't even prove my innocence. To this day, they believe I set the fire and never considered anyone else. The only reason they didn't fry my ass was because, while I failed to provide a concrete alibi, they failed to produce any real proof." She inhaled a shaky breath. "Oh, and let's not forget during this I found out I carried that cowboy's baby. Oh yeah, rumors flew. That's why I stayed with an aunt who, by the way, couldn't stand the sight of me." Her body shook, and she inhaled a noisy breath. "How's that for facts! I was minutes away from not even being able to attend my parents' funeral."

The embarrassment, the confusion, the frustration of no one believing her fisted a tight hold on her chest as if it were yesterday. Her heart beat loud in her ears, and she fought to get air. She could see the officer standing over her, yelling at her, asking her where she had been that night, asking her why she set the fire, why she killed her parents. A mix of emotions clogged her throat, terror of no one believing her, fear of being locked up for a crime she didn't commit squeezed the oxygen from her lungs.

"Breathe slow."

Jordan's vision cleared, and Trent came into view. "Oh, God." Mortified over all she said, she covered her face with her hands.

"When you keep things bottled up, you're bound to explode," he commented in the gentlest, quietest tone, pulling her fingers away.

"You didn't deserve that." Ashamed for lashing out and not quite sure what to do or how to back up the last few minutes, she focused on the ground.

"I'm a big boy. I can take it."

A large man, yes he was, but a boy? No way. She regarded him through drooped lashes and chewed on her lip to keep from chuckling. Her being able to laugh right now proved how screwed up her life had been, at least to her.

A calloused finger lifted her chin. "If I could change anythin', it'd be the fact I let you leave that morning." Eyes closing, he ducked his head and nipped her lips.

The horses pranced, throwing her off balance. She grabbed his shirt front to keep from falling.

A low, guttural moan sounded as Trent slipped a hand under the weight of her hair, holding her, ravishing her lips, pulling her up half out of the saddle.

A moment ago, she was close to the breaking point, but now the feel of him grounded her, making her feel out of control for a totally different reason. The man had an uncanny ability of putting her on a roller coaster. He pulled her to sanity when she was on the brink of disaster. She leaned further into him, seeking more, wanting the warmth he offered to ward off the nightmares. Desire spread like liquid fire.

He broke the kiss and rested his forehead on hers.

Realizing she was halfway laying across the back of the horse—her foot still caught up in the stirrups—she righted herself and settled into the hard leather seat.

"Damn," he muttered, then reached over and tucked a strand of hair behind her ear.

She closed her eyes as a shiver flirted with her

nerve endings.

"Ready to finish this ride?"

In a daze, she nodded and mechanically nudged the animal's sides then, eager to free her mind, she galloped off toward the barns.

The wind whipped through her hair, caressing her face. No matter how many times she rehashed the past, the events stayed where she wanted them…in the past. Yet, sharing those humiliating teenage years with Trent made her chest lighter.

Seeing the buildings in the near distance, Jordan slowed Champ to a steady walk as Lucifer appeared at her side.

"Thank you," Trent drawled.

Confused, she glanced his way. The heat of his gaze made a fuzzy feeling start in her head. "For what?" Coming to the front of the barn, she reined in the horse.

"For being honest and clarifying a couple of things." He gave her one of his sexy grins, then broke eye contact.

Emotions tied in knots, and not wanting to end up falling on the ground, Jordan concentrated on dismounting.

"If you tie him to the hitching post, I'll untack him when I finish with this guy," the cowboy informed her.

"I can do it. I'm not a greenhorn." She loosened the cinch.

"That you definitely aren't." He positioned his roan-colored gelding to the other side and smiled. "Have at it, m'lady."

Chuckling, Jordan set about her chore, all the while admiring the way his muscles bunched under the tight

T-shirt. Not once had he favored his shoulder during their afternoon together—

"Mr. Trent! Mr. Trent! I need you," a high pitched voice cried.

Peter sprang from one foot to the other in the doorway.

"What's up my man?"

"I need your help. I can't find my pa, and my ma…the baby's hurtin' her real good. You gots to help. I don't know how to make the baby stop. Please, Mr. Trent."

Setting the horses loose in the pasture, he lifted the child into his arms. "Jordan, I may need your help."

Needing no further encouragement, she hurried to keep up with his long gait.

Peter tucked his face in the crook of the cowboy's neck as the three rushed to the cabin.

"I tried to help, but my ma, she told me to go find someone and bring 'em back," he cried.

"It's okay, buddy. You did good. We'll help your ma. Everything'll be okay." Trent glanced back at her with a plea in his eyes.

Jordan sent up a silent prayer. From what Peter told them, Mrs. Parker was most likely having contractions. Giving birth was trying enough, but add an early delivery into the mix and they could be facing a whole plethora of problems.

Going over the scenarios in her mind, she hoped for the simplest answer—the woman was experiencing Braxton Hicks contractions. But as they advanced onto the porch and heard a moan from inside, her hopes diminished.

Trent set the boy on the porch. "You stay here and

keep watch for your dad, okay?"

"Y-yes sssir."

The kid's eyes were huge as saucers and his face pale. If it wasn't for her nurse's training, she'd send the cowboy in to see to Mrs. Parker alone, and she'd stay right here to console the child.

"Mrs. Parker, you okay?" Trent asked as he neared the spot where she slumped on the floor.

"I seem to be in labor. I honestly...oh..." She clutched a towel in her hand and inhaled several breaths before finishing. "This one's early."

The fear on both faces impelled Jordan to step into gear. "How far apart are your contractions?"

"Couple of minutes."

"We have some time," she assured the woman, then turned to Trent, widening her eyes, hoping he'd understand the urgency. "Call for an ambulance."

His gaze flew over the patient, then back to Jordan. He blinked several times as if he couldn't believe what was going on. "And if they don't get here on time?"

"Then we'll have to deliver this baby." *Please, God, don't ask this of me.*

The cowboy's face lost all expression, and under other circumstances, she may have found the situation comical, but right now, right here, having to deal with her own demons, a wave of nervousness churned her stomach.

Swallowing the bile rising, she knelt and wiped her sweaty palms on her jeans. "How far along are you?"

"Thirty-three weeks."

Okay, not too horribly early, but still—

"*Oh...*" the woman groaned.

Trying to keep track on her watch, Jordan waited

out the contraction and calmed her own skittering nerves by listening to the deepness of Trent's voice as he explained the situation to the operator on the phone.

"Contractions are three minutes apart," she told him, hoping to light a fire under someone's backside at the emergency department.

He relayed the message, then swore. "I lost signal."

"What?" *Please let me have heard him wrong.*

"Happens around here sometimes. They have the address anyway."

She glanced to the patient and noted wetness on the floor. "Get some clean towels, her water broke."

While he gathered the cloths, she struggled to help Mrs. Parker stand and strip off her pants. "Let's get you on the couch."

"Here." Trent dropped an armload of towels on the end of the cushion, glancing from the patient to Jordan.

"They're getting closer." The woman shut her eyes and squeezed the back of the sofa.

"What would you like me to do?"

Make the ambulance appear outside. "You ever deliver a baby?" She strode to the sink to scrub her hands.

"Livestock, yes, ma'am. A human, nope, can't say I have."

"Go check on Peter. Try to call one of your brothers. Maybe they know where Mr. Parker is."

As he left, she positioned herself back at the guest's feet. "Breathe, Mrs. Parker. Try to relax your body."

In all her years of nursing, Jordan had never delivered a baby other than her own, and for that reason, she relied more on memory from her own pregnancy than her training. She turned the mother-to-be on her side and rubbed the bottom of her back through another contraction.

"You're doing great." When the pain subsided, she rolled her back over. "I'm a registered nurse," she shared with as much confidence as she could muster. "I want you to bend your knees. I need to check your dilati—ah, Trent, I need you. *Now*."

"Something wrong?" the patient asked in an alarmed voice.

"No, ma'am. This baby's just in a hurry." She smiled, trying to ease the woman's fears.

Her knight in shining armor appeared, losing color when he took in the sight of the baby's head crowning. He shook his head and stared in Jordan's direction. "Chris doesn't know where Mr. Parker is, but he's going to look around. What do you need?"

"Mrs. Parker—"

"Please call me Martha," she panted. "Seems silly...to keep with the formal...*oh*."

"Breathe, Martha. One, two, three. Trent, support Mrs. P—Martha's—back, and let her rest against you."

The brave cowboy scooted into position.

"Give her your hand."

He moved without a word, his gaze fixated on Jordan's face. The respect and trust shown in his eyes gave her the boost in confidence she needed to see this to the finish.

"Martha, do you have a bulb syringe I can use to suction the mucus from the baby's mouth and nasal passages?" she asked, waiting for her patient to take a cleansing breath.

"In my bag. It's by the door. I like to be prepared,"

she spat out. "Oh, God, where's Roger?"

"That your husband?"

"Yesss," the woman hissed through her teeth.

"I'm sure he'll be here soon," Trent's quiet, calm voice assured her.

Despite the raised brow and slight frowns he cast Jordan's way, he gained control of himself, while her own nerves increased toward the panic mark, and she fought to stay in control.

"Not soon enough...*Oh...I need to push...*"

Hurrying, she located the needed items. "Okay, you ready to have this baby?"

Please, let everything be okay. Please, let this miracle come into this world without any problems, she chanted over and over in her mind as she guided the infant out of the birth cannel, stopping the mom a time or two in order to clean the mucous from the mouth and tiny nostrils.

"It's a girl!" She laid the baby on the mother's stomach and waited for the small person to take her first breath. The stillness of the night rang loud in her ears as she made another feeble attempt at cleaning the airways.

"We'll take over, ma'am."

A palm touched her shoulder. Realizing the paramedics arrived, she rose to her feet. Anxiousness filled her chest as she crossed to the sink and washed her hands. She barely finished drying when the shrill cry of a newborn split through the room.

"Thank you," she whispered and went out the door to check on Peter. Her foot barely swept across the bottom step when she spotted him a couple of feet from the cabin.

"Congratulations, you have a baby sister."

He glanced up with crocodile-size tears in his eyes. "I want my dad."

Kneeling down to the boy's level, she pushed aside her own turmoil and reached out. These things had to be scary to a young child. "I'm sure he'll be here any minute." She grasped his hand in hers. "Come on, I'll wait with you."

Together, they went to wait on the porch as the door opened. The paramedics pushed Martha and the new baby on a gurney toward the ambulance. The whole scene was surreal. This was the first time she'd participated in a delivery since her own baby had been born. The feel of the small, warm, slippery body in her hands caused them to shake now in the aftermath of the ordeal.

She took a deep breath, her chest heavy and tight, leaving her to wonder if the ache would ever go away.

Peter let go of her hand and ran toward a tall man and young boy approaching from the right.

Mr. Parker stopped in his tracks, lifted the child, his head swinging from one person to another. The poor man appeared scared out of his mind when he spotted his wife being loaded into the vehicle. Giving his son a hug, he set him next to his brother and hurried toward the ambulance. He kissed his spouse, and then the bundle lying on her chest.

Jordan heard Trent offer to keep the boys for the night in order for the couple to spend time at the hospital, but the man refused, piling the two kids and various items into his vehicle.

Not ready to talk about the events, she hurried to her own bungalow, anticipating a long, hot shower before having to face her cowboy again. Despite the warm night air, her hands and feet felt like ice cubes.

Opening the door, she kicked off her boots and stripped down on the way to the bathroom. Turning on the water, she stood under the hot spray, willing the images of her own lost daughter to recede. This wasn't the first time she dealt with an infant, but it was her first birth.

Working at the hospital, being around babies had always been hard, but she managed to brush aside her feelings and do the best job possible, waiting until she arrived home after her shift to breakdown. She had seen heartache, and some fates much worse than hers. People triumphed every day over their misery and fears. Why couldn't she do the same?

The strange part was, being here on this ranch, around Trent, gave her an inner peace she'd been lacking. The concern, for her, in his eyes every time she glanced up from delivering the Parker baby had moved her. He'd given her the strength to see Martha through the ordeal.

She often wondered what her life may have been like if her parents hadn't died. Would she have continued her wild ways, or would she have grown up? Would her baby have made it? Would she have found Trent? Would her life be happy, fulfilled?

Didn't matter much now. The facts remained. They did pass away. She did lose her baby. She had found Trent. And she was a twenty-four-year-old with no plan.

She realized her misconceptions over how she dressed or who she kept company with had little to do with letting her parents down and more with her own guilt over enjoying life, while they had lost theirs.

Six years was long enough to wallow in self pity. Her mom and dad *would've* wanted her to be happy. Maybe it was time she stopped punishing herself, because frankly, she was tired of it.

And if she was completely honest, not knowing much about the cowboy who showed her understanding and tenderness left her feeling a bit deflated. Being here, getting to know the man himself, truly captured her heart.

The events of the past replayed in her head as they had many times before, but this time, she stopped fighting the memories and embraced them until the water ran cool.

****

Trent grabbed a garbage bag and placed the soiled linen inside, then picked up miscellaneous items from the floor before mopping the area. Cleaning up the Parker's place took no time at all, but he hoped the few minutes would be enough for Jordan to clear her head, because he needed to see her, if only to reassure himself she was okay.

After the ambulance drove away, he turned to ask her how she was holding up only to see her sprinting away toward her cabin. She'd been a real trooper, jumping in and delivering the newest member to society. But the ordeal must have prompted a great deal of sorrow. He could only imagine how difficult tonight had been for her.

As many times as Trent watched animals being born, nothing compared to a human life. To imagine Jordan going into labor alone, without her parents or him, then to deliver a stillborn drew a knife into his heart.

Hurrying to his cabin, he grabbed a bottle of whiskey before continuing to Jordan's door. The wood stood open, and the boots she wore lay on the floor, but he received no answer when he knocked.

Opening the screen, he let himself in. A path of clothes led to the bathroom, which he found odd. She didn't strike him as the messy type. Everything else in the place was neat and organized. Alarm drove him closer to the door. Hearing the water shut off in the shower, he breathed a sigh of relief.

Trent made his way to the cupboard and extracted two glasses, filling them half-full of whiskey. He sank onto the couch and waited for Jordan to come out. Minutes later, she opened the barrier, steam billowing out behind her.

Drying her hair with a towel, she turned toward him and jumped.

"What are you doing here?" She tugged the thin, white, knee-length robe closed tighter.

"Checking on you." He stood and crossed the room.

"I'm fine."

He studied her freshly scrubbed face, and the longing to hold her was too great. Grasping her upper arms, he rubbed up and down in a slow, rhythmic motion. "Aren't we past the lying game?"

Confusion shown in her gaze, and he knew she struggled with the notion of letting him in, letting him get close.

All at once, the fight drained out of her, and she sagged against his chest.

Not sure who needed the comfort more, he

wrapped her in his arms, swaying back and forth. "Wanna sit?" he asked after a few moments.

Without answer, she shuffled over to the couch.

"Come here." Lowering himself, he swiveled with his back on the arm of the sofa and positioned her between his outstretched legs.

"I'm okay, really. I was cold when I got home and couldn't get warm. The hot water helped."

"It's seventy-some degrees outside." How could she possibly be cold?

"I think I had a bit of anxiety coming on."

"Here." He pushed her up an inch or two to claim the glasses on the coffee table. "This might help."

Jordan sipped the brown liquid and coughed. "What the heck is that?"

"Whiskey. Sure way to chase the chill away."

Eyes watering, she placed the back of a wrist to her mouth. "Thanks."

He chuckled. "Guess I should've warned you."

"It's okay. I forgive you." Smiling, she swirled the liquor. "You know, for the first time, I let myself relive all that's happened in my life. Going over and seeing each incident take place, step by step." She twisted to one side. "I've always blocked the memories, thinking the pain would be too much, but then I remembered the fun times with my parents, the talks my mom and I would get off on. She really loved me. They both loved me."

"How could they not...I mean, they're your parents." He sipped...or guzzled the drink. No way did he mean to imply he loved her. Like, yes, but he wasn't ready to mistake that for more...again.

"I couldn't see that before. And the baby, there was

nothing I could have done. I ate fruits and vegetables, even ones I hated. I took my vitamins. I went to my doctor appointments."

Trent wanted to point out he tried to tell her all this, but kept his mouth shut. She'd accomplished a peacefulness with her past, and that's what he wanted.

"The one thing bugging me most—was you."

"Me?" She lost him on that statement.

"Yes, you. I didn't know where you lived or even who you really were. I needed closure with the fact I slept with a stranger, the closest person to a true friend. I shared more with you regarding my life than any other human being, yet I was unable to find you." She downed another sip of whiskey.

"You found me now," he whispered in her ear, then scraped the lobe lightly with his teeth.

"Yes, I did." Jordan snuggled into his chest, rubbing the wetness from her hair into his shirt.

But it wasn't the damp cotton distracting him. "You really need to stop pushing your backside against me if we plan on holding much more of a conversation."

She wiggled again, precariously close to his straining erection.

Hands itching to touch her, he finished off the alcohol and leaned over to set the cup on the table. "You're askin' for trouble, darlin'."

She giggled and flipped her head back on his shoulder.

Not able to resist, he stroked the opening seam exposing her breasts. "What exactly do you have on under this thing?" Running the back of his knuckles up and down, he grazed the sides.

"Mm. I love when you touch me." She raised an arm behind her, curling a hand around his neck.

His pulse leaped as his groin tightened. He planned on talking with her more, but with her whispered admission, the thought process was lost, and any rational conversation done.

Wanting a taste of her, he nipped and suckled the side of her throat, tasting the salty skin, smelling the soapy fragrance, feeling the erratic beat of her pulse at the base of her neck. He let his hand wander down her body to where her thighs parted and separated the cotton robe. Without breaking contact with his lips, he let his eager hands explore her from collar bone to thigh, breast to breast, lightly caressing, then squeezing, exploring the depths and mounds.

Jordan's whimper encouraged him, egging him on. Trent circled his tongue around her ear and trailed his fingers to the soft juncture between her legs, skimming lightly over the opening. "You're so soft and silky, like satin."

When his thumb grazed her clit, she raised her hips, thrusting into his palm. "Please."

Not able to deny her plea, he slipped into her warm center, and stroked her. "Is this what you want?" Her sleek wetness met his fingers, and with his other hand, he nudged her limbs farther apart, opening her to his assault. He ran his fingertips up and down her inner thigh as his other continued its massage of her internal muscles. He loved seeing her aroused, the drooping of lids, lips parting as she escalated.

"Yes." Her breath quickened, and she rotated in a restless gesture, bucking in his palm.

Sensing the rising urgency, he slipped another digit

inside while using his thumb to play with the swelling nub. The massive erection in his jeans strained to be freed.

She lifted her bottom half-up, rocking in rhythm with him, riding the whirlwind. "Yes...please...Trent." Her nails scraped his denim-covered thighs.

The beauty of watching her searching, reaching for the finish was almost his undoing. And when her organism spiraled, he fought hard to contain his own.

A second later, he slipped out of her, tenderly brushing the swollen skin.

She rose, letting her cover fall to the floor. "Your turn, cowboy." Shaking fingers unfastened his belt buckle and hurried on to the zipper.

Oh, hell, yeah. He was about to explode.

Operating under due haste, he helped shed the clothing and freed his eager penis. She sank to her knees beside the couch and grasped him in her palm. Her tongue flicked the tip, and he grew stiffer. The black-haired beauty was like a sexual fantasy, taking him into her mouth, licking up one side and down the other with her tongue. Sucking and retreating until he was sure he'd spill over.

He held back, and rigid with restraint, he groaned, tangling his fingers in her hair, holding her still. "For a woman of little experience you...certainly know what...the hell you're doin'." He panted as her tongue lashed out, licking the beaded tip.

Glossy lips smiled, lifting off him. "Reading is my favorite pastime."

"What the hell kind of books do you read? Much more of that and it's all gonna be over in a matter of seconds."

She rose over him, lifting his shirt up overhead, rubbing her nipples along his torso.

Unable to take any more, he reversed positions. She was hot and exotic laying on the cushions, openly waiting.

"Don't move a muscle. I'll be right back."

Hurrying to the other room, he grabbed a condom from the bedside table, slid it on and returned, quickly finding his place. With one push, he buried himself deep within her, leaving them both breathless.

"Damn. I wanted this to last." Unable to hold back, he withdrew and plunged back in, creating the hot, fast friction he sought.

Long, toned legs wrapped around his waist, and she met him thrust for thrust as he drove into her.

Need and pure hunger propelled him faster toward the edge. His mouth found her nipples, licking, suckling, biting each taut pebble until she exploded a second time. He quickly followed, shouting her name.

Chapter Twelve

Early the next morning, Trent rolled on his shoulder, sending a searing burn straight to the bone.

"I told you not to carry me to bed." Jordan bunched the covers under her arms and rose halfway. "Let me help you."

"What kind of man would I be if I can't carry you?" He moved forward while she positioned herself behind his back.

"A healing one."

Magical fingers worked into the tissues bit by bit, and he closed his eyes, blocking out the discomfort until the muscles relaxed. Having not much more than tenderness the past few days, he'd assumed the surgical site was finally mending. *Damn. One step forward, two steps back.*

"Better?" Her sweet voice surrounded him.

"Yes."

Warm lips caressed the skin on his back.

"When are you going to tell me what happen?"

"Rotator cuff surgery. Not a big deal." He scooted to the edge of the bed in search of his clothes. Where were they?

"That explains one scar. What about the other?"

"What time is it? And where the hell are my clothes?" he snapped, suddenly pissed at her for bringing up that part of his life.

Her eyes widened at his tone as she slid down on the mattress. "It's eight o'clock, and they're probably in the living room."

"I'm gonna have to get a damn alarm clock if I spend much more time here." He placed a chaste kiss on her cheek and hurried out of the room.

Why did she have to go and ruin the mood after spending another blissful night together?

Because she doesn't know what happen, you jackass.

He didn't want to relive those days with April, didn't want to subject Jordan to his ugly past. The future was what mattered now. Not the pain and hurt, the deception and manipulation, the humiliation.

Taking a chance on seeing pity in her blue gaze was not an option, so he charged out of the cabin and up to the barns. Regret for leaving in a rush and biting her head off for asking a legitimate question settled in. Why couldn't she leave his scars in the past where they belonged?

"Hey there, can you help me?"

Trent spun on his heels to find a brunette dressed in a small, black tank top and equally tight shorts, standing behind him.

"You're Trent, right?" She smiled, revealing straight, white teeth.

"What can I do for ya?" Upon closer examination, he noted her height to be an inch or two shorter than his. Not hard on the eyes with shoulder length, shiny hair, and a slender body with curves in the right places.

"Would it be okay for me take a horse out for a ride?" She crossed and uncrossed her long legs.

He pushed his Stetson back on his head. "Sorry,

but we don't allow the guests to ride unsupervised."

"Well, you could go with me, then I wouldn't be unsupervised." She bowed her head, glanced up sideways, and smiled. "I'm Pam by the way."

Trent knew a come on when he heard one, but only one woman sparked his interest these days, and he'd be lucky if she was still speaking to him. "I have a full day, but I'm sure one of my brothers are free."

Her bottom lip stuck out in a pout, but he paid no mind and glanced around to find Chris not far away. "Hey, this young lady would like to go sightseeing. You game?" he hollered.

"Sure thing." The horny bugger strutted over with a grin from ear to ear. "It'd be my pleasure, ma'am." He displayed his elbow in a gallant gesture, earning him a giggle from the brunette. "But first, we need to get you out of those shorts and into a pair of jeans. Can't have those beautiful legs chafing."

Pam giggled again.

Shaking his head, Trent continued with the day's work, not stopping to question why he possessed no interest in any of the women on the ranch. Except one.

The hours flew by as he engrossed himself with ranch chores and helped guests untack the horses from the camping trip with Nick and Darcy before his stomach grumbled over a skipped lunch. Forced to head to the house for supper, he wasn't sure if Jordan would be there or not. At the least, he owed her an apology for his rudeness. When she asked of his injury, old defenses rose, and he hadn't wanted April to tarnish the moment.

"Hey, I was on my way to find you," Sam told him as he entered the main lodge.

"Why aren't you headed for Tulsa?" Trent hung his hat on the peg next to the door.

"On my way out now." His brother's gaze bore into him. "April's on the run."

Instant cold ran up his spine. *"What?"*

"What?" Nick and Darcy asked in unison, walking into the room.

"The chief of police called, said they aren't sure how, but April escaped from the psych ward sometime during the night. He assured me they'll find her, and figure out how this could have happened, but wants us to be on alert."

Trent knew they waited for a reaction, but numbness surrounded him as he poured a mug of coffee. "Maybe she skipped town." He hoped like hell that was the case. The alternative was too disturbing to think about.

Sam stared at him, his lips pressing into a thin line. "Doubtful. When the nurse went in to her room this morning to give her breakfast and meds, she found pictures of you and letters addressed to you scattered on the bed."

Chris entered the room and stopped in his tracks. "What's the long faces about?" He pointed toward Trent with a jerk of his thumb. "You reminding him chores start at six a.m." His chuckle filled the room. "You spend much more time in Jordan's bed, you're gonna have to make an honest woman out of her."

Choking on the hot liquid, he wiped his mouth with the back of his hand. "I don't think so."

"What's that suppose to mean?" Darcy questioned with a frown.

"Nothing. Never mind." He charged toward the

table and set his cup down.

"You mean my friend's good enough to sleep with, but not to consider marrying?" She crossed the room until the tips of her boots met his. "Don't you use her, Trent Matthews. She's suffered enough with the last asshole and doesn't need her heart broken by you."

"Calm down, darlin'. I don't think that's what he meant." Nick placed his hands on her shoulders and rubbed. "Is it Trent?" he asked, scowling.

"He's only saying he isn't ready to propose," Chris defended.

"His last engagement left the kid gun shy," Sam added.

Trent placed his hands on the table and leaned forward. "Are ya'll done discussin' my life?"

All eyes bore down on him. Feeling cornered, beads of sweat broke out along his forehead. But even with everyone gawking at him, he refused to say anything he hadn't even contemplated in his own mind.

"*If* I ever decide to get married, the engagement will be a long one, and that's a big *if*. I don't plan on making the same mistake twice. And while I enjoy spending time with Jordan, I don't plan on walking down the aisle—"

The door banged shut, drawing everyone's attention.

A dark blue gaze slammed into him harder than the bullets that had pierced his skin.

Jordan stepped back, blinking rapidly. One arm went around her midsection as her sights drifted sideways toward the others.

"Jordan, I—"

Whirling on her heel, she flew back out the door. A

second later, he heard a vehicle start up.

"Aren't you even going after her?" Darcy asked, her annoyance clear in the tight tone.

He rubbed the base of his neck where the tension started. "Maybe one of ya'll should, since ya apparently have my life all figured out."

"You need to talk to her. Don't you think you owe her that much?" His future sister-in-law poked a finger in his chest.

"Sweetheart, let it go." Nick grabbed her hand.

Trent closed his eyes to shut out the noise. *"I'd give her the moon, if I could."*

Jordan's smile flashed in his mind. The way she brushed her hair back from her face. The way she cared for Peter and held the precious life she helped deliver. The soft sigh as she slept, and those sweet little sounds she made when she snuggled into his chest.

"Damn." Grabbing his hat, he kicked the door open. The last thing he'd wanted to do was hurt her...again.

****

Jordan possessed no idea where she headed, but needed to get away. A little time to suture up the gash Trent sliced into her heart. Not that she'd expected a proposal tomorrow, but his words hurt. Plain and simple. And in front of his whole family to boot. She'd be the first to admit they needed time to explore the relationship, but hearing him put a stop to any fantasizing at all was like slamming the door in her face.

And what did he mean about making the same mistake twice?

Once again, pieces of his past he neglected to

share. The one man she desired, the one she cared for—loved—closed himself off.

Tears clouded her vision, and she swiped at her eyes with the back of her hand. The vehicle suddenly hit a pothole, hard, jarring her body and almost causing her to swerve off the road. Slowing, she noted the thump, thump of a blown tire.

Forced to pull over, she wiped the remaining wetness off her face with shaking hands. A beep sounded from the passenger seat, and seeing a text from Darcy, she picked up the cell phone.

U ok? Where r u? Please come back so we can talk?

I'm fine. Went 4 a drive 2 clear my head & put things in2 perspective. B back b4 2 long, she typed, then pushed the Send button. Almost immediately, the device sounded again, indicating a voice mail. Not sure when she missed a call, she hit a few buttons and held the mechanism to her ear.

"Hello, Jordan. This is Dr. Sheffield. I was calling to let you know there's a part time position opening up within the next few weeks. If you want it, the job's yours. Now, I know you were hoping for full time, but it's a start, and as fast as things change around here, you'll be working sixty hour weeks before you know it." He chuckled. "Call me back."

Jordan hit the End button again and groaned. Now what? She had to take the job of course, but there was no way she could remain on the ranch or work there now. Which meant she'd need to find an apartment in town and another job until the alleged sixty hour weeks started. Maybe a waitress job. They made good tips.

She ran a hand through her hair. *Damn it.*

Frustrated, she threw the phone back on the cushion. She sure as hell couldn't stay here all night. Praying the rental had a spare, she glanced out the window for oncoming traffic before edging the driver's door open. A big truck slowed and pulled up behind her. A tall cowboy with a low riding black hat climbed out of the cab. If she hadn't recognized Trent by the outline of his body, the slow swagger would've been a dead give away. Not ready to deal with him, she rested her forehead on the steering wheel.

The door opened all the way. "Car trouble ma'am?"

She lifted her head, but stared out the windshield. "Nothing I can't handle."

"Looks like ya blew a tire. These roads can be rough."

Inhaling, she made a move to exit the vehicle, but his big body blocked the path.

Trent bent, removed his Stetson, and placed the hat on her lap. Warm hands bracketed her face before his mouth caressed hers.

Hands fisted on his chest, she was ready to shove him away, but instead found herself clinging to his shirtfront. Those inviting lips soothed her battered soul, making thinking impossible. He kissed her with more tenderness than she'd ever known. He make her feel treasured and loved.

"Please, stop. This isn't going to help." Mustering the strength, she dragged her mouth away and glanced down the road, wishing for someone to come along to keep her from giving into temptation. Much to her dismay, they seemed to be the only travelers.

"We need to talk."

"We can't very well carry on a conversation on the side of a highway."

"This is an old logging path. I only knew to go this way because Charlie was outside and saw you make the turn."

Great. Even when she wanted to get lost she couldn't.

Jordan glanced at him, then out the windshield, seeing nothing but dirt and trees. "I'm leaving the ranch in the morning," she blurted.

He blew out a noisy breath. A warm palm caressed the back of her head, then guided her cheek to his chest.

She felt the rapid beat of his heart and shut her eyes, savoring the feel of him one last time.

"I've held a lot back and hurt you in the process," Trent said in a rough voice, one full of emotion. One she'd never heard before.

He raised her face and stared into her eyes. "But that wasn't my intention. I figured the past was better forgotten."

Jordan waited, wanting to hear more, wanting him to tell her, but he volunteered nothing further. God, she wanted to hit him. "After everything I've told you and all we shared, why can't you open up to me?"

He stood staring at her until she fought the urge to scream.

"Forget it. If you can't tell me even now, this is just over." She shoved his hat at him and pushed past. Going to the back of the vehicle, she found a small jack, a tire iron, and a half-decent spare under the bed.

"Let me." Trent tugged the jack from her hand and set to work on the tire.

Jordan shook her head. "I can do it."

"Please. We need to talk, and the sooner we get this done, the sooner we can straighten things out."

She whipped her head his way. "And are you going to talk, Trent? Are you going to trust me enough, as I've trusted you? Or do you think sex will make up for everything?" She was aware her voice rose and was thankful no one else was around.

He stood and slid her hair back behind her ear, sending a jolt through her body. She held herself ramrod straight, refusing to give him the satisfaction of knowing how he affected her.

"I'll tell you anything you want to know."

Not quite believing him, she raised one eyebrow.

"I swear."

Seeing nothing but honesty in his open arm stance, she nodded. "I'm telling you, Trent Matthews, if you hand me a line of bullshit, I'm leaving...for good."

"Duly noted, ma'am." He placed his Stetson on her head and set about changing the flat. "Looks like you ran over some type of metal." He pulled the object out of the sidewall of the rubber. "Must have been sticking out of the road. Certainly is an odd angle to get wedged into."

Jordan inspected the piece he handed her. A metal nail file? How on earth had that happened?

"Maybe it was in there a while, and hitting that divot punctured the tire further." He tightened the bolts and put everything away. "That should do it." Opening the driver door, he gestured for her to get in.

Sliding past him, making sure not to touch in any way, she sat behind the wheel and stared ahead. "Thank you."

"My pleasure, ma'am."

She heard the smile in his voice and glanced up at his face. A calloused finger stroked the side of her cheek, and she had to steal herself against the desire to close her eyes.

"Follow me?" he asked.

Knowing she'd never forgive herself if she drove away without answers, she simply nodded and watched him climb into his truck.

The smell of him lingered in the cab of her vehicle. His Stetson on her head left her dizzy with what it implied. She knew most cowboys didn't give up their hat easily. So what did it mean? For most, it signified she was his, but for others, the act meant nothing. Right now, she could not be his, and the self-inflicted pain made it difficult for her to breathe. She switched on the radio to drown out the nagging voice in her head.

Dusk fell quickly as she kept up with his taillights, cursing herself for being every sort of fool. His turn signal flashed, and she followed suit, but halfway down the dirt drive, recognition shocked her. This was the way to the shack.

The place contained too many memories for her to remain objective, yet she wanted his explanation, needed to hear the words come out of his mouth.

At the end of the path, she parked beside him and debated what to do. Staring out the windshield, she caught a glimpse of a shadow moving toward the trees, but the only thing in sight were a couple of squirrels.

Her driver side door opened.

"You gettin' out?" A note of edginess lined Trent's tone.

His nervousness gave her momentary pause and a sliver of confidence.

"Yes." Shutting off the engine, she stepped from the vehicle and followed him inside their shack.

"Hopefully, the lantern still works. I'd even settle for a few candles. It's gonna be pitch black out here soon." He rummaged through the two cupboards and produced both. Setting the lamp on the table, he switched the knob, but nothing happened. He flipped the object over and tinkered with the battery.

"If you give me the candles, I'll light them while you mess with that thing." She placed his hat on a peg on the wall and extended her hand.

"There should be matches in the drawer."

Not giving into the strong urge to glance his way, she found the matches and lit the wax.

"The terminals are corroded." Trent pulled out his pocket knife, scraped the remnants off the battery, and reassembled the pieces before he flicked the knob. Light sputtered, then illuminated the room. "You can blow out the candles. We'll keep 'em close by in case the lantern doesn't last."

Jordan glanced around. The cabin appeared clear of debris and cobwebs. A total contradiction to their last visit. Maybe that's why he brought her? To show her and remind her of the time they spent together? "You cleaned the place up."

He shook his head. "Wasn't me, but someone obviously has."

"Maybe Darcy and Nick snuck away to be alone."

"Don't see why when they have their own place." Tension radiated off him, and she wondered what his stress was all about.

Not really caring who tidied up the space, she shrugged and doused the wax sticks.

He grasped her hand and motioned for her to sit on the cot, then lowered himself next to her.

His lips brushed hers and half of her melted. The other half rose in defense. "Huh-uh." She extracted herself from his arms and scurried to the end of the bed. "You promised we'd talk."

"We will."

"Now."

He blew out a breath and scooted over until the wall supported his back. Raising one knee, he rested his forearm across the bone. "What I said back at the house had nothing to do with you—"

"Sounded like it had everything to do with me."

"Do you wanna listen or argue?"

His tone remained light, yet she sensed his uneasiness, and instead of answering, zipped her lips, for now.

"I care about you a lot more than I've ever cared for a woman…but I'm nowhere near ready to marry."

Hurt blazed in her eyes, and Trent felt the pain of disappointing her all the way to his soul. He rushed on to explain. "I'm not saying this very well." Needing contact, he intertwined his fingers with hers. "All through high school, I dated this girl, April. We had an on again off again relationship. My buddies and some of the girls at school warned me she was crazy. I figured they meant as in wild, havin' a good time type crazy, but as time went by, I realized she wasn't stable, mentally. Anyway, we broke up a few times over the course of two years and—"

"Were you dating her the night you and I—"

"No. That was one of the broken up times. But she figured I was hers forever. She approached me,

163

claiming she loved me and how I hurt her by being with another girl. She knew you and I spent the night together, 'bout the skinny dipping and everything. She made me feel guilty. She was upset, but different, like she really missed me, and we started dating again. She promised to take her medications and see a psychiatrist. Everything appeared better." Resting his head on the wall, he wondered how to explain why he asked April to marry him. His reasoning sounded lame, laughable even as he compared his feelings for Jordan to what he experienced back then.

"I didn't love her. I know that now, but I felt responsible for her, like I pushed her too hard and maybe made her be the way she was. It seemed like the right thing to do at the time, what was expected." He peered into those blue, blue eyes, holding her gaze, hoping against the odds she'd understand. "So I proposed. A couple of weeks later, her apartment complex burned to the ground. She had nowhere to go, and we planned on getting married anyway, so I asked her to move in with me. One thing led to another, and we fought all the time. Mind you, this went on over a period of almost four years. She complained to everyone who'd listen how I neglected her and spent too much time dealing with the ranch, but the final straw came about two years ago, when I agreed to go out of town to pick up a bull for my brother. When I arrived home, all hell broke loose."

Not sure what she thought, he fidgeted, and played with her fingers. "She accused me of going to see 'Jordan.'" He examined her features, gauging a reaction. "I told her I didn't know who this Jordan was, but she called me a liar, pulled out a pistol, and shot me, twice."

The full realization of April knowing *Lynn's* real name hit him like a ton of bricks. Somehow, the witch discovered the information that would've changed his life. An eerie feeling crept down his spine. April had been more deceitful than he gave her credit for.

"Oh, my, God. That's why the scars and the surgery?" She wrapped her arms around him in a fierce embrace. "She shot you because of me."

He grasped her upper arms and pulled back. Tears shimmered in her eyes. "Do you understand? I knew her for years, yet she was more of a stranger to me than you were that night."

Needing to feel her close, he snuggled into her hair, inhaling the intoxicating vanilla scent when something whacked his arm, and she withdrew.

"Ouch. What was that for?" He rubbed the spot.

"Don't you ever compare me to that monster." Small hands shoved at his chest.

"No, darlin', that's what I'm trying to tell you. When April got upset and angry, I turned away." Trent took a hold of her fingers and brought them to his lips. "When I see pain in your eyes, or when I think you're upset or crying, I want to hold you. I want to make you better. You aren't *anything* like her, and my feelings for you are far stronger, but it's me." Perspiration beaded on his back. He had to make her understand. The thought of losing her bore too much heartache. "I need to take things slow."

"Same bottom line if you ask me."

He cupped her chin. "Nowhere close." Lowering his head, he grazed her lips once, twice, before crushing her to him. She tasted like coffee and sunshine, and he wanted more. He wanted whatever she was willing to give.

She wrenched away. "Did you hear that?"

"What?" Nothing penetrated over the pounding of his heart. He held on, afraid she'd walk out if he let go.

"Listen. There it is again."

Something smacked the side of the cabin, then the door flew open to reveal the one redhead Trent had prayed he'd never see again.

Chapter Thirteen

"Well, well, well, isn't this cozy."

"April, what are you doing here?" Staring at the end of a pistol, Trent shuffled toward the edge of the bed, careful to keep Jordan behind him as the door slammed shut.

"Don't move, you two-timing dirt bag," she yelled. "I came back to be with *you*, and you're with *her* again. How could you do this to me?" A wave of anxiety entered her voice as she eyed Jordan with distain. "And you, why couldn't you have died like you were supposed to. Damn you, Trent, always coming to her rescue."

Jordan inched closer to his side.

Rage filled him. Was she admitting to trying to kill Jordan? He forced himself to be calm and speak in a level tone. "What do you mean, she was supposed to die?"

"In the fire, damn you. Or today. She could've at least had the decency to land in the hospital after her tire blew out. Damn it, why do you always go back to her?"

Catching a glimpse of the cell phone in Jordan's hand, he decided to keep the crazed woman talking. "You're the reason she got a flat?"

"So smart cowboy." She stepped closer. "But if she would've died in the fire, none of this would've happened." Her eyes narrowed in Jordan's direction. I will never forgive you for seducing my fiancé."

"What fire?" Trent stood to keep April from the bed.

"And here I called you smart. The night of Charlie's bonfire, when *she* refused to leave with her slut friend, who by the way will give you any information you want if you get her drunk enough." April laughed. "I discovered little miss tramp's real name, and where she lived…" She shook her head. "I tried giving you a chance to explain, but I couldn't find you after your skinny dipping episode. So, I decided to pay your girlfriend a visit myself and set her damn house on fire. Only later, when I came back, she was still sleeping right here *with you*!"

Jordan gasped, and the sound ripped him apart. He couldn't imagine the pain the sudden confession must be causing her, but he couldn't soothe her right now. Not if he wanted to save her.

"There's something about those flames, the way they light up the night and burn everything in their path. I love watching the destruction. It's like wiping the world clean of sin." Her face light up with a crazy happiness as the corner of her mouth twitched. "I may have failed the first time, but I don't give up. I'm no quitter. I spent too much time planning everything to have this whore ruin it all," she hollered, waving the gun in front of her. An evil smirk encased her lips. "Burning down my apartment building got you to let me move in, and I made sure I did everything right to get you to propose." She stood taller, pushing her breasts out as if she were proud of her accomplishments, then anger flashed in her eyes,

168

transforming her features to reflect cold, malicious fury. "If you could've just stayed away from this tramp." The pistol dipped, then rose.

He trekked closer.

"Stay right there." Shadows danced around the room in the lamp light as the gun wavered in her hand.

April was more of a loose cannon than he'd ever imagined. He had to get Jordan out of here.

"For a while, I thought it'd work out." April snarled. "Then you started talking about black hair and blue eyes in your sleep."

Behind him, Jordan jerked up. If he wasn't clear on how much she meant to him, surely this would convince her.

"I wanted to choke you with my own hands. I'd lie awake at night listening to you sing her praises—do you know how sickening that was? And when you deserted me to pick up your precious bull, I knew you were going to see her. That's when I decided if I couldn't have you, no one could."

A vacant look came over her face as she stared straight at him, and he wondered if she'd shoot him in this very spot without any warning. He braced himself, waiting, praying he'd get the chance to tell Jordan how much she meant to him.

April's shoulders slumped a bit, and she sniffed. "I didn't want to shoot you, honey, but you gave me no choice."

"It's okay…sweetheart." He swallowed the bile in his throat at the endearment, but figured their only hope was to play along, and hoped like hell Jordan knew what he was doing. "I forgive you. I understand, and it's not too late. We can be together now." He gentled his voice to distract the delusional woman and keep her attention on him. "You and me. We can go anywhere you want. I know how much you hated the ranch. We can have a fresh start somewhere else."

April stared, her eyes softening. "Really? You'd leave your family for me?" A frown grew as her features took on a hard edge. "No. You're lying. I've been watching you with her. What is she doing?" She moved forward and motioned for Trent to move aside. "Get out of my way."

He held his ground. No way was he letting her close to Jordan.

She pointed the pistol at the center of his chest. "I said move, cowboy."

"No. Don't." His black-haired beauty skirted around his back and held out her phone. "Here."

"Aww. How sweet of you to protect your lover, but really stupid of you to attempt calling for help." She snatched the device out of her hand and waved the barrel of the gun. "I should shoot you right here."

Trent sidestepped to block her path, prepared to feel the blow pierce his skin, again, but the pain never surfaced.

April stomped her foot. "To this day you're protecting her. Does she mean that much to you that you'd give up your own life?" Her voice rose with hysteria. "*Why?* Why couldn't you love *me* that much? I gave you everything. *Everything.*" Tears ran down her cheeks as she walked backward toward the door, opened the wood, and threw the phone out into the black night. "If you can't love me in this life, maybe you'll love me in another."

His mind went crazy trying to figure a way out of

this. "Can't you forgive me? I'll spend the rest of my life making this up to you." He tried one more time to convince her of his intentions. "What can I do for you to believe me?"

"Tie her up."

Trent glanced to Jordan's confused, pale face and back to the evil witch standing way too close. There had to be a way out of this. "What?"

"You heard me."

"Why?"

"Then we can go outside and watch this place burn…with her inside. The flames are even more impressive in the dark." Confident laughter filled the cabin and sent a cold streak down his spine. Not lowering the gun, she reached her other hand to the waistband of her jeans and tossed him a couple of small ropes she'd had tucked there.

Two pieces of twine smacked him in the torso and fell to the ground. "Can't we just leave her here?"

"No." Anger filled her features. "Tie her up…or I'll shoot you both." She pointed the pistol at him, then Jordan.

Fear for the woman he loved forced him to pick up the line, hoping like hell he'd be able to protect her from the raving lunatic. Turning, he moved in slow motion, trying to stall. Needing to find a way to reassure her he'd get them out of this, his eyes met hers, and the fear in her features ripped his heart in two.

"And no funny business. I *will* check the knots."

"I'll get you out of this baby," he whispered to Jordan, leaning into her, pretending to wrap the rope around her wrists. "Grab the knife in my front pocket and be ready. When I say go, *run* out that door." As his lips brushed her warm, smooth cheek, he felt her grasp the switchblade.

She set the stiletto under her leg and shook her head; the tears brimming her eyes weighed heavy on his heart. If she only understood, with her out of harm's way, he'd be able to disarm April. He hoped.

He swiped a knuckle over her cheek. "For me, please."

"Hey, no talking. What's taking you so long? Let me see that knot."

He needed a couple more seconds. "Just finishing."

"Do her feet, too."

Trent ran a hand down to her ankle, embracing Jordan's leg. "I mean it," he mumbled. Hearing a creak, he angled his head and noted the door opening. He coughed to cover the guest's entrance.

"Hurry up." April moved closer, waving the gun in his face.

A shadow emerged through the entrance at the same time Trent finished. Timing it just right, he jumped up and knocked the pistol from her hand as his oldest brother grabbed April from behind. The firearm fell to the floor with a thud, and he bent to retrieve the weapon, tucking the gun in the back of his waistband.

"You, asshole." April spat out at her captor as she kicked at him. "Don't you know what he did to me? How he cheated and hurt me?"

"I know you tried to kill my brother once before, and I wasn't about to let you do it again." Anger filled Nick's tone as he jerked her arms behind her back.

Trent untied the loose ropes from Jordan's ankles and wrists, then tossed it to his brother.

April kicked and bucked, trying to break free. The

pair ended up sprawled on the floor. Nick flipped her onto her stomach and began securing her with the rope. She swung her feet backward almost knocking him sideway.

Trent hurried over and grabbed her legs.

His brother glanced back. "Thanks. She's a wiry little bitch."

"Give me the other rope." Taking the twine, he tied her ankles together. He didn't know how his brother knew, but was sure thankful he showed up. "Thanks," he told his sibling.

"Didn't want Mom and Dad to have to call their vacation short for your funeral," Nick joked without smiling and cupped him hard on the shoulder.

"Ow, damn you." He moved his sore limb and chuckled. With the danger over, he felt like a weight was lifted off his chest.

April glared at the three of them, spitting and sputtering profanities.

"Will you shut up already," his brother yelled.

Realizing Jordan hadn't said a word, he crossed the room, grasped her hands in his, and pulled her to her feet. She stared over at the crazy woman on the floor, and Trent nudged her chin up with a finger. Her eyes were wide, but she smiled, giving him all the encouragement he needed. Not able to stand any distance between them, he slid his good arm around her narrow waist and pulled her tight to his chest. Lowering his head, he brushed her lips with his for what was meant to be a quick kiss, but one taste was not enough. Pressing his mouth fully onto hers, his tongue swept in, tasting sweet heaven.

A throat cleared. "Hey, can you two save that until

after we get this one in police custody?"

Reluctantly, Trent pulled back and faced Nick. "How'd you know where we were anyway?"

He nodded toward Jordan. "She texted Darcy. Four words: shack, April, gun, help. I was headed over the ravine on my way back from a trail ride when Darc called me. Wasn't too hard to figure out. Lucky for you, my horse knows this area well enough to travel in the dark."

Trent hugged Jordan tighter. This time he got it right, this time he fell in love with an amazingly smart lady. Yep, he was one lucky man.

"You stupid bitch. You will pay for this," the mad woman hissed.

"You're the only one who's going to pay." Trent informed April.

"I didn't think the message went through. I couldn't get signal," Jordan mumbled.

"The signal was plenty strong, *if* you choose to receive the message." His brother caught his eye and winked. "I'm going to take this one outside to wait for the police. I had Darcy call them. They should be here any second."

He watched him haul April out the door, then pressed his forehead to Jordan's. The nightmare was finally over. Now, all he wanted was to go back to his cabin and hold the love of his life all night long.

"You okay, darlin'?" He ran his palms up her arms and to the sides of her cheeks to reassure himself.

Jordan couldn't believe all that happened and couldn't seem to find her voice. Her heart beat wildly in her chest and her hands trembled, but she managed to nod her head, then hid her face in the front of Trent's shirt absorbing his strength.

"Shh. You're okay."

His masculine voice washed over her as his palm smoothed over the back of her head. How could he be so calm? The crazy woman had killed her parents. All these years, Jordan took on the blame, and this nutcase was the murderer. She balled her fingers into his shirt, making fists. All the guilt and heartache, the pain she suffered, all because this deranged lunatic wanted to keep her from Trent.

And April planned on killing her, too. Thankfully, her hero stopped that from happening, putting her out of harms way over and over. Even standing in front of the loaded weapon. She sat on the mattress and looked up at the most courageous man she knew. "She...she killed my parents."

He picked up his switchblade from the cot and placed it in his pocket, then enclosed her hand with his warm one.

"And she was going to kill me?"

"I wouldn't have let that happen."

Trent glided a finger along her chin; his love-filled gaze caressed every inch of her face.

No, he wouldn't. He proved that by stepping in front of the pistol. He'd give his own life for her. The potency of that realization shocked her. This man, who couldn't commit to marrying her, was willing to die to keep her safe.

"I love you." The words tumbled from her lips before she could stop the flow. "Oh, God. I didn't mean to say that out loud." Silence filled the air. Fearing his reaction would be worse than facing down a gun crazed ex-fiancée, she stood and would've darted across the

175

room, but he grabbed her wrist. "Forget I said anything." She prayed someday his mind would accept what his heart already showed her.

Sitting on the edge of the mattress, his hands slid to her hips and pulled her to stand between his legs. "Do you know how scared I was when I thought I might not get a chance to tell you? How scared I was to say the words?"

He rested his forehead on her belt buckle for a second, and she leaned over, pressing her lips to the back of his head. "It's okay. You don't have to say anything you aren't ready to."

Dark eyes met hers, as he rose. "Thing is, I didn't think I was ready for any of this." He laughed. "But this last half-hour—"

Did they really only come to the cabin a half-hour ago? Felt like hours to her.

"I couldn't stop thinking how much you mean to me, how my feelings for you are so different from any other." His grip tightened on her hand. "Jordan, I'm not ready to propose, but I am ready to love you, to erase all the hurt, to make new memories, more explosive than the first ones. And someday, I *will* marry you, because I plan on spending the rest of my life with the woman I love."

"Wh-what are you saying?" Her chest grew heavy with anticipation, and she didn't know if she wanted to laugh, cry, or slug him.

"Jordan Lynn Reece, I can truly say without any reservation, I love you, and someday we will be married," he repeated. "For now, I'd like to build on what we've started, that is, if that's what you want, too?"

She threw her arms around his neck. "I want that very, very much." Staring into the warmest brown eyes, she said around the lump in her throat, "Mr. Trent Matthews, I love you. I always have, and I always will."

Not able to wait any longer, she kissed his lips. Somehow this man who showed her understanding and tenderness as a teenager, came back into her life and offered her love and forever. And she knew now, deep in her heart, her parents would be happy for her. It only took one hot, slow-swaggering cowboy to show her it was okay to be herself.

She stared into his eyes. Dreams she thought gone forever were now mapped out in his tender gaze. The explosive heat they shared one night six years ago had erupted into a love so great she looked forward to every day of their future together.

A word about the author...

Sherri Thomas has always loved country living, from the animals on a ranch to the cowboys who care for them. Throw in a good romance and that's why she became an author. When she's not reading or writing a romance you can find her caring for her many animals with her own cowboy and four children.

She can be reached at:

http://sherrithomas.blogspot.com

or http://facebook.com/SherriThomasRomance

or follow on her on twitter

http://twitter.com/sherlynromance